SAMANTHA SPINNER

AND THE

BOY IN THE BALL

BOOKS BY RUSSELL GINNS

SAMANTHA SPINNER

SPINNER

AND THE

BOY IN THE BALL

RUSSELL GINNS

ILLUSTRATED BY BARBARA FISINGER

A YEARLING BOOK

This is a work of fiction. Names, characters, places, and incidents either are the product of the author's imagination or are used fictitiously. Any resemblance to actual persons, living or dead, events, or locales is entirely coincidental.

Text copyright © 2020 by Russell Ginns
Cover art and interior illustrations copyright © 2020 by Barbara Fisinger

All rights reserved. Published in the United States by Yearling, an imprint of Random House Children's Books, a division of Penguin Random House LLC, New York. Originally published in hardcover in the United States by Delacorte Press, an imprint of Random House Children's Books, New York, in 2019.

Yearling and the jumping horse design are registered trademarks of Penguin Random House LLC.

Visit us on the Web! rhcbooks.com

Educators and librarians, for a variety of teaching tools, visit us at RHTeachersLibrarians.com

The Library of Congress has cataloged the hardcover edition of this work as follows:
Names: Ginns, Russell, author. | Skorjanc, Barbara Fisinger, illustrator.
Title: Samantha Spinner and the boy in the ball / Russell Ginns ;
illustrated by Barbara Fisinger.
Description: First edition. | New York : Delacorte Press, [2020] | Summary: "After finally finding Uncle Paul, Samantha realizes her brother Nipper is now missing and must find him. But while hunting him down, she must elude the mysterious and nefarious CLOUD that's hot on her heels"— Provided by publisher.
Identifiers: LCCN 2019018172 | ISBN 978-1-9848-4919-9 (hc) | 978-1-9848-4921-2 (ebook)
Subjects: | CYAC: Adventure and adventurers—Fiction. | Brothers and sisters—Fiction. | Missing children—Fiction. | Uncles—Fiction. | Family life—Fiction. | Mystery and detective stories.
Classification: LCC PZ7.G438943 Sad 2020 | DDC [Fic]—dc23

ISBN 978-1-9848-4922-9 (pbk.)

Printed in the United States of America
10 9 8 7 6 5 4 3 2 1
First Yearling Edition 2021

TO CAROLE KARP:

I share your passion for words and history.
I share your enthusiasm for learning about the world.
Thanks, Mom!

The Gateway Arch

In St. Louis, Missouri, the Gateway Arch curves proudly beside the Mississippi River.

At 630 feet, it is the world's tallest arch, the tallest monument built by humans in North America, and, of course, the tallest structure in the city. Completed in 1965 as a monument to westward expansion in the United States, the arch is an instantly recognizable symbol of St. Louis and a major tourist attraction. The observation deck provides an excellent view of the surrounding city and far beyond.

The Corn Palace

The Corn Palace in Mitchell, South Dakota, is a public arena. Hockey games, concerts, and conventions take place inside—surrounded by corn!

The outside of the building is covered with real corncobs and corn husks. Local artists use them to create colorful murals. Updated almost every year, the corn creations showcase farming, music, sports, geography, and highlights of American history and culture.

* * *

Both of these landmarks are located above entrances to the *hoverdisk highway*. Standing on a disk that floats on a cushion of air, you can zoom through the highway's underground tunnels like a puck gliding on an air hockey table.

Successful hoverdisk operation requires a combination of balance, quick reflexes, and precise computation.

Depending on your skill, you can cruise under the Great Plains at speeds of up to three hundred miles per hour. Of course, it's very important to pay attention to low-clearance warnings. Watch out for the HEAD!**

** Horizontally Extending Architectural Dangers

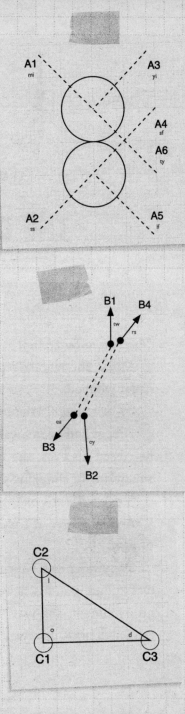

CHAPTER ONE

THE BAD SEED

"Bird brain! Bird brain!"

Missy Snoddgrass's parrot was still squawking. It never stopped.

"Waitaminute! Waitaminute!"

Nipper had been awake the entire night. Every time he closed his eyes, the horrible bird started talking or squawking or shrieking again.

"Let's roll! Let's roll!"

And, of course, it's hard to fall asleep inside a big ball of yarn.

Everything had happened so fast. One moment he was standing in his living room, talking to Missy. The next moment, she was rolling him head over heels up the Snoddgrass driveway in a massive yarn ball.

"Pajama Paul! Pajama Paul!"

After finally finding Uncle Paul with his sister Samantha, Nipper had had to rush home from New York. His dad had signed him up for calculus camp: Camp Pythagoras. It was an unbreakable contract, and if he didn't show up on time, there would be trouble. Nipper wasn't looking forward to five weeks of calculator karaoke, algebra art projects, and long-division dancing. The trigonometry time trials sounded just awful. But getting trapped in a ball of yarn where you couldn't move your arms or legs was even worse!

He couldn't see anything but yellow wool. And it was really itchy.

"Yankees lose! Yankees lose!"

Nipper was tired, sore, and hungry, and, worst of all, his Yankees really needed him. While she wrapped him up in yarn, Missy had swiped all the New York Yankees player contracts . . . again. She had snatched the deed to Yankee Stadium . . . again. Somewhere out there, beyond the yarn, his Yankees were on a one-hundred-game losing streak, and he was too tied up to do anything to save them.

"Watch out for the —! Watch out for the —! Watch out for the —!"

"Jeremy Bernard Spinner," called a voice. "Stop bothering my bird. You're going to wear her out."

Through a gap in the yarn, Nipper could see the yellow-polka-dot blouse Missy Snoddgrass always wore.

"Come on, Missy," he pleaded. "I've been stuck in here all night. I feel like my head's about to explode."

"Thanks for your words of encouragement," she replied. "I'm trying to set the record for the world's biggest ball of yarn or string or twine."

"Those are three different records," said Nipper.

Through a gap he saw her shadow circling. He figured she was still adding to the ball.

"And you're not even close," he told her. "All three records are more than ten feet in diameter."

"I know, I know," said Missy. "And I'd probably get disqualified anyway because there would be a dead boy inside."

Nipper gulped. He didn't want to find out if Missy was joking or if she really meant it about the dead boy. There had to be a way to escape. He shifted his weight and rocked the ball back and forth a little.

"Stop that," said Missy.

Nipper felt her grab the ball to hold it still. He spotted some fingers through the yarn. On one of them, she wore the emerald scorpion ring he had given her months ago. The green gem flashed.

"Tell you what," she said. "I'll let you go if you give me something I want."

"You already have my baseball team," said Nipper. "Nothing's more precious than that."

"Well . . . your uncle is always giving away interesting presents to you and your sisters," she said.

"I've got two toy cars—and some stickers," Nipper replied, eager to make a deal. "I also have a weird spoon, an old silver dollar, and a really fancy pocket watch."

He struggled to twist his body as he spoke, but the yarn held him in place.

"Let me go and you can have all of it," he pleaded.

Missy's shadow disappeared and reappeared. He hoped she was walking around him, considering his offer. Polka-dot fabric appeared again, very close to him now.

"I'm not interested in stickers, spoons, or watches," said Missy. "But what about that *umbrella* your sister drags around? I'd like to get my hands on that."

"Samantha's not here," said Nipper. "She's still in New York City, and she's with—"

He stopped himself. He was pretty sure Sam wouldn't want him to discuss their adventures. Especially with someone who was double-triple super-evil.

"She'll be back in a few days," he said.

"Fine," said Missy. "I can wait. I'm a very patient person. When your sister comes back, I'll let you go."

"When she comes back?" Nipper cried. "I said *a few days!*"

A strand of yellow dropped in front of his left eye. It reminded him of mustard. That reminded him of hot dogs.

"And I'm getting hungry," he whined.

"Hungry?" she asked. "I can help you with that."

Through the yarn, Nipper could see her reaching into the front pocket of her blouse. She pulled out her hand, reached up to the ball, and slapped the gap in the yarn near his mouth. Little round, dry bits came flying in. He licked his lips. Crunchy . . . but not much flavor. Seeds?

"Hey!" he shouted, spitting them out. "This is . . . this is bird food."

"Oh. So now you're a picky eater?" asked Missy.

"*Picky eater! Picky eater, picky eater!*" squawked the parrot.

In the distance, a doorbell rang. Missy leaned in close.

"You're going *no place*," she whispered through the yarn.

Nipper heard her walk up the side porch and into her house.

He really needed to get out of there. He shifted his weight and tried to make the ball rock again.

"*No place! No place!*" screeched the horrible bird.

CHAPTER TWO

BYE, GEORGE

George Spinner stood on the Snoddgrass front porch. He counted in his head. This was the fifth time he had been there in the last twelve hours. He rang the Snoddgrass doorbell for the nineteenth time.

"Nipper?" he called. "Are you in there?"

The lock turned and clicked. The front door creaked and began to open very slowly. Young Ms. Snoddgrass stared at him through the screen door. She wore the same pleasant smile as the last four times he had been there.

"Hello again, Mr. Spinner," she said sweetly. "It's always nice to get another visit from a good neighbor."

"Of course," he said. "But I'm *still* looking for Nipper."

"Jeremy?" she asked. "He's still missing?"

"Yes," said George. "But I hired you to be his baby-sitter. Weren't you the last person to see him?"

"Last person. Last . . . night," Missy said slowly.

She seemed to be remembering things.

"Well, when we heard the sound of your car arriving, your son asked me to leave him alone," she explained. "He told me he wanted time to clean up the house for you and to spend some quiet moments studying mathematics before bed. Of course, I honored his wishes."

"You heard my car coming?" asked George.

"Yes," she answered.

"He wanted to clean up the house and study math?" he asked.

"Yes," said Missy. "He was such a calm and thoughtful child. He will be missed by everyone."

Mr. Spinner scratched his head. There was something odd about all this.

"He put himself to bed?" asked George.

"Yes," said Missy. "I checked in on him before I left. Sleeping like a little angel."

"Hold on," said Mr. Spinner. "I went to wake him up this morning, and he was gone. I found a big pile of socks and balled-up newspapers under his sheets. Are you sure you didn't—"

"Have you told Dr. Spinner about this?" Missy Snoddgrass asked before George could finish.

"Suzette? No . . . not just yet," said George.

He massaged his forehead with his fingers nervously. He hadn't spoken to his wife since yesterday. That was before their son vanished.

"I'm waiting until I find Nipper first," he said.

"That's very smart of you," said Missy. "Very good. Dr. Suzette Spinner would probably be very upset if she found out you lost one of her children."

George nodded. They had spent a lot of time in New York reviewing strategies on how not to lose track of things or let the house get destroyed.

"You don't want your wife to be worried . . . or *really, really mad*, do you?" Missy asked.

George shook his head. The odd young woman definitely seemed to understand the situation.

"Do you want everyone in your family to think you're careless, forgetful, and unreliable?"

George shook his head three more times.

"Maybe . . . it's a better idea to call *Samantha*," she said slowly. "Samantha can come home and help you search."

"Excellent suggestion," said George.

Maybe it hadn't been a mistake to hire her as a babysitter. She was definitely a smart young lady.

"Good," said Missy, smiling at him. "Good . . ."

Out of the corner of his eye he could see her reaching for the doorknob. Then . . .

"Bye!" Missy yelled, and she slammed the door.

George stood on the porch for a minute, reviewing everything Missy had told him. Then he turned toward home.

"There's at least one flaw in that young woman's story," he said as he walked to his own front door. "My electric car doesn't make any noise."

CHAPTER THREE

INTERRUPTED VANISHING PERSON

Samantha went looking for Uncle Paul.

He was somewhere in Buffy's apartment.

She had fought off ninjas, traveled from France to Italy to Indonesia to Peru to Mali, tracked her uncle down in New York, and saved him from clowns. Now, finally, she was going to learn *everything*.

Samantha was going to learn all about the Super-Secret Plans. How did all those pictures and diagrams get inside the umbrella? Why did her uncle give it to her? What exactly was PSST, the Partnership of Super-Secret Travelers? What was the story behind that amazing map room she and her brother had found in Peru, under the ruins of Machu Picchu?

Samantha let out a long, satisfied breath. After all the adventures, mysteries, and clues, Uncle Paul was here. And *she* was here, too. Now she was going to make the most of it.

Nipper and her father had already gone back to Seattle, but Samantha had an extra day in New York City. She had to go sit through her sister's foolish play again that evening, but she still had all morning and afternoon to spend with her uncle . . . starting now.

Samantha rode the escalator to the top floor, past paintings of gloves and scarves. Diamond-encrusted handbags and platinum-plated high-heeled shoes shimmered in glass cases.

When she reached the landing, she took a moment to gaze through the panoramic windows of Buffy's three-story penthouse sky castle. Then she surveyed a dozen more shoe statues, purse paintings, and glittering gloves.

Far across the ridiculous room, a pedestal supported a gleaming tree-shaped sculpture, about as tall as a person. She squinted and took a closer look. Eight golden branches sprouted from a tree trunk. A silver horseshoe dangled from each branch.

Someone stepped out from beyond the sculpture.

She smiled.

It was Uncle Paul.

He had his back to her, and he was facing the wall, looking at a painting of two sailing ships.

"*Pursuit*," said Uncle Paul, reading the brass name-plate at the bottom of the picture frame.

"Yes," said Buffy, appearing in the doorway. "Isn't it awful?"

She was wearing her Egyptian fairy-tale princess costume again. Sapphires twinkled on her silver headdress. Samantha noticed that, other than some streaks of plaster dust from last night's theater battle, her sister matched the decor of the room perfectly.

"I hung it on the wall to warn all my new employees not to mess up," said Buffy.

"Employees?" asked Samantha as she joined Uncle Paul in front of the painting.

"Yes," said Buffy. "I need new ones, now that Nate's all gone."

"You mean Nathaniel?" asked Samantha. "The pirate?"

"All gone?" asked Uncle Paul.

"I wanted a painting of a purse-suit," Buffy whined. "You know, a *suit* made of *purses*."

"Sometimes you need to take a closer *listen* to things," said Uncle Paul.

"So," Buffy continued, ignoring her uncle, "I asked Nate for help."

"An accessory to accessories," said Uncle Paul.

"I get that one," said Samantha, smiling at him.

"Of course you do," said Uncle Paul.

"What-ever," said Buffy, waving her hands to get them both to look toward the picture. "My useless assistant brought me that thing instead."

Samantha leaned in to inspect the painting. One ship, flying a skull-and-crossbones flag, fired cannons and chased after the other ship.

"Wait, go back," she told Buffy. "Did *you* decide that this picture is a warning, or did someone else tell you that?"

"Stick around," said Uncle Paul. "I'm about to tell Samantha some important things about exciting places . . . and some terrible dangers."

"Borr-ring," said Buffy.

"Oh, come on!" Samantha blurted. "Aren't you curious about all the crazy mixed-up things that keep happening to us? How about the amazing presents from Uncle Paul? Don't you want to know where your two point four billion dollars came from?"

"Ignorr-ring," said Buffy.

She turned and headed to the exit.

"I changed my mind," she called back over her shoulder. "When you're done talking about nonsense, take the painting down and drop it off at the Metropolitan Museum of Art."

"Museums don't just let people *drop off* paintings," said Samantha.

"Well, they should," said Buffy. "Museums should celebrate purses and suits."

When she reached the doorway, she stopped and looked back at Samantha and her uncle.

"And footwear," she added thoughtfully. "There should be a whole museum dedicated to the magic and wonder of shoes."

Buffy turned and walked out of the room.

"Your sister sure has vision," said Uncle Paul.

"Yeah," said Samantha. "Double-triple super-bananas vision."

"Not exactly," said Uncle Paul. "That's something different."

Samantha wondered what her uncle could have possibly meant by that. Then she realized they were alone again. Here was her chance.

"Okay. Right now," she said, putting her foot down harder than she intended.

The silver horseshoes on the tree jingled.

"Tell me every single detail. Put all of them in order, and start from the very beginning."

"That is definitely one of the ways you can tell a story," said Uncle Paul.

"Begin, please," said Samantha, impatient to get the story started.

Finally, he cleared his throat and began:

"Two hundred and thirty-two years, five months, three weeks, and six days ago . . ."

"Hello, Paul," said Samantha's mother.

Samantha hadn't noticed Dr. Spinner come into the room.

"Good morning, Suzette," Uncle Paul said cheerfully.

Samantha didn't turn. She kept watching Uncle Paul. He had just started from the beginning, and she didn't want to miss anything.

"And good morning to you, too, dear," said her mother.

Samantha didn't move.

"Dear?" Dr. Spinner asked.

Samantha still didn't move. She hoped her mother was just passing through on her way to somewhere else.

Her mother sighed. "It's all clear, Penelope," she called. "There are no Komodo dragons in here today."

"That's a relief," Aunt Penny said, walking into the room. She carried her shopping notepad as usual. "Thanks for checking."

Samantha watched as her aunt looked up at the ceiling and started scribbling.

"Buffy sent me in here to inspect the gold-plated ceiling," Aunt Penny explained. "She says it's scratched, so she wants my help to replace the whole thing with solid platinum."

"Sometimes you can buy a lot with a *Penny*," Uncle Paul whispered.

Samantha smiled and nodded at him. He was right about that. Aunt Penny was a professional shopper and treasure hunter . . . and Buffy's personal glitz gatherer.

"What are you two up to now?" her mother asked. "Are you talking about WRUF again?"

"The Worldwide Reciters of Useless Facts, Mom?" asked Samantha. "No. That's not important. We're about to talk about some super-secret—"

"*Plans* are an important part of every adventure," Uncle Paul interrupted. "Don't you agree?"

Dr. Spinner looked at Uncle Paul, then at Samantha, then back at Uncle Paul.

"All right," she said, turning to Aunt Penny. "Let's leave so-mysterious and so-serious alone for a while. I'll go with you to explore ceiling solutions."

"Thanks, Mom," Samantha called as her mother and her aunt left to gather their things.

"You must be so-serious," Uncle Paul said, walking over to the grand piano in the center of the room.

He sat down at the bench, leaned forward, and examined a piece of paper. Then he sat up straight and started to play.

"You can put lots of notes together and make a masterpiece," he said, turning to look directly at Samantha.

He smiled and kept watching her as he played.

Uncle Paul seemed to be waiting for her to figure something out.

She shook her head.

"Must you be so-mysterious?" she asked.

She went to the piano and picked up the page in front of her uncle. It was a sheet of music printed with gold ink. The words *SCARLETT HYDRANGEA'S SECRET OF THE NILE PART TWO: THE UNICORN RETURNS* glistened on it.

Samantha frowned, turned the page over, and set it down on the lid of the piano. That was definitely not part of any *masterpiece*.

"Didn't you say you were going to tell me something really important?" she asked.

"I did," said Uncle Paul.

"I want you to tell me everything," she said. "All the facts."

"I'll do that, too," said Uncle Paul.

He swiveled on the piano bench to face her, his eyes opened wide. Samantha was ready.

"Over two hundred years ago, there was only . . . the WEATHER," he said.

He raised his hands and began to waggle his fingers as he spoke. "Of course, super secrets can also be used for super-evil schemes."

Samantha smiled and settled in. Her uncle was such a good storyteller—once he really got going.

"If you explore the world and take a closer look at things, you'll find there are secrets and possibilities—everywhere!"

He really got going.

"We have many places to go and a lot to—"

Suddenly he jumped up and spun around.

Samantha was so focused on hearing everything, she hadn't even noticed that her mother had reappeared and had tapped Uncle Paul on the shoulder.

"Sorry to interrupt again," she said.

She held out her phone toward Samantha.

"It's your father, dear," she said.

"It's Dad?" asked Samantha, exasperated. "We're busy. Can't it wait?"

"I don't know, dear," said her mother. "I'm not sure why, but he doesn't want to talk to me. He only wants to talk to you."

CHAPTER FOUR

GOODY, TWO SHOES

Samantha sighed and took the phone from her mother.

"Hi, Dad," she said. "I'm really busy right now. Would you mind calling back after I get a chance to hear about the—"

But her father started talking, and she couldn't get a word in. He rattled on about lightbulbs, the Space Needle, Nipper, calculus camp, his super-quiet electric car, and not-Nipper.

"Stop," she interrupted. "What's *not-Nipper*?"

"Exactly," said her father. "Your brother is gone."

"It happens all the time, Dad," said Samantha. "You know that."

"Yes, of course," he said. "But I've searched every-where."

"Been there, done that," said Samantha.

She really had been everywhere with Nipper. And losing and finding and losing and finding him had been a big part of that whole experience.

"I believe you," said Mr. Spinner. "But he's been gone for a long time now, and I'm really getting worried."

"Okay, okay," said Samantha.

Her father definitely sounded more worried than she had ever heard.

"I'll ask Mom to help figure out what we can all do about it."

"No-no-no!" her father said quickly. "Don't do that. I need *your* special talent."

Samantha looked at her mother, smiling and waiting patiently. Then she looked over at her uncle. He still had his storytelling hands in the air.

"Can I bring Uncle Paul with me?" Samantha asked.

"Yes. That would be good," said her father, sounding happier. "Extra help would be useful—just not your mother."

Samantha smiled. This was her opportunity to spend time alone with Uncle Paul—without these constant interruptions.

"Okay," she told her father. "We're on our way."

Samantha clicked the call off and handed her mom's phone back. "We've got to go back to Seattle immediately," she said.

"Immediately?" asked her mother, clearly surprised. "What about Buffy's play?"

"You've seen one theater full of clowns, you've seen 'em all," said Samantha.

Uncle Paul nodded approvingly.

Dr. Spinner shot both of them annoyed glances.

"Fine," she said. "I'll go change your plane tickets . . . again."

Samantha watched her mother march out of the room. Then she turned to Uncle Paul.

"I'll grab my purse and my suitcase," she told him. "And the Plans."

"I'll wait right here," he said, standing up from the piano bench.

Samantha eyed him carefully: rubber boots, green plaid pajama pants, tuxedo T-shirt.

"Don't you have anything you need to pack?" she asked.

"Not really," he answered.

Samantha smiled. She liked her uncle just the way he was.

"I could bring the top hat I took from that angry clown," said Uncle Paul. "It had a boxing glove inside, remember?"

Samantha nodded.

"But . . . no," he added. "It doesn't go with my pajamas. Too formal."

"Okay," said Samantha. "I'll be right back."

She took the escalator down to the "guest room" two floors below. Buffy had put Nipper and her in a stable built for the rainbow unicorns she planned to buy someday. Samantha scrounged through the pile of shredded newspapers her sister had provided as a bed.

"Gotcha," she said, lifting an old trombone case from the mound.

She found her purse and looped it over her shoulder. Then she grabbed her suitcase, which she'd never unpacked, and a minute later, she was back in the living room with a case in each hand.

"A musical instrument?" said Uncle Paul, eyeing the trombone case. "You're full of surprises, too, Samantha."

She set down her suitcase, unsnapped the trombone case, and opened it just enough to show the red umbrella inside.

"Aha! Now you're getting it," he said. "Super secrets survive concealed in commonplace containers."

"Thanks. Wait . . . what's that supposed to mean?" she asked.

Samantha heard her mother coming back. She closed the case quickly.

"I changed the plane tickets for you," Dr. Spinner announced.

"Thanks, Mom," said Samantha.

"And, Paul," Dr. Spinner said. "George called again while I was on the phone with the airline. He wanted me to let you know that he has the dog clogs ready."

Uncle Paul froze. "What?" he asked quickly.

"I'm pretty sure he said 'dog clogs,'" her mother replied.

Samantha thought she saw Uncle Paul's hands tremble slightly.

"Dog . . . clogs," he said slowly.

Samantha couldn't figure out what had come over him so suddenly. He'd gone silent and was standing completely still. Finally, she clapped her hands twice to get his attention.

Uncle Paul didn't respond. He continued to stare off into space. Then, he slowly tilted his head and stared up at the gold-plated ceiling.

"Button," he whispered.

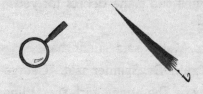

CHAPTER FIVE

DOWN AND OUT

Samantha walked with her mother toward the elevators on the top floor of Buffy's sky castle. Every now and then, she looked back to make sure Uncle Paul was there. He still seemed dazed, but he kept following them.

In the foyer, she saw her sister blocking the main elevator and waving for them to use the freight elevator.

Samantha shook her head. She walked straight up to Buffy, reached around her, and pressed the button for the main elevator.

"Please don't make us go through the loading dock, Buffy," she said. "Someone's in trouble, and I've got to go find them."

"Again?" asked Buffy. "Doesn't that happen to you *all* the time?"

Buffy looked at Uncle Paul. She studied him for a moment. Then waggled a finger at both of them.

"You two make excellent traveling companions," she said. "A roving fashion disaster."

Samantha didn't have time to feel insulted. She set down her cases and handed her sister a piece of paper.

"This is really important," she said. "I made a list of playgrounds, stores that sell stuff with Yankees logos, and things that could fall out of an eight-year-old boy's pockets. I need you to call Dad and read it to him."

Her sister nodded silently.

"Word for word," Samantha added.

Buffy nodded again.

"I mean it," said Samantha. "I need your help to—"

The main elevator chimed, and pink marble doors slid open.

"Let's go," Samantha told Uncle Paul, stepping around Buffy.

"Hold on," said Aunt Penny.

She held out a *Secret of the Nile* tote bag and reached inside.

"I was out shoe shopping for Buffy, and I saw these in a discount bin."

She held up a pair of brand-new orange flip-flops.

Samantha watched as her uncle stepped out of the big rubber boots, took the flip-flops from Aunt Penny, and quickly put them on. He drew a long slow breath and let it out again. Then he smiled at his sister.

"Thank you," he said.

He looked over at an oversized, gold-plated, gem-encrusted garbage can, on the floor by the far wall. He tossed the boots one after the other into the can.

Samantha stepped toward the elevator.

"Wait," he said to Samantha. "Let me help you."

He picked up her suitcases and walked past her, into the elevator.

"Have fun," said Aunt Penny.

"It's a shame to see you . . . go!" Buffy called.

Samantha ignored this last insult from her sister. She just hoped Buffy would follow her instructions.

"Tell your father to call when you're all together at home," said her mother.

"I will, Mom," said Samantha. "Thanks for everything, Aunt Penny."

She stepped into the elevator next to Uncle Paul and turned back to her sister.

"Don't forget, Buffy," she said. "I am serious about the list. It's really important."

Her sister held up the page and waved it at her. She was still waving it as the elevator doors closed and Samantha and Uncle Paul began their descent to the first floor.

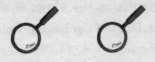

CHAPTER SIX

BROADWAY OR BUSTED

"When Sammy departs, the party starts!" Buffy announced.

She balled up Samantha's paper and tossed it into the sparkling wastebasket with Uncle Paul's boots.

"Tonight is ladies' night," she continued. "And all of the Spinner girls will go to the theater together."

"All?" said Dr. Spinner. "Your sister just left for Seattle."

"Yes," said Buffy. "'*All* of the Spinner girls' is so much better when it doesn't include Samantha."

"That's a little unfair," said Aunt Penny.

"Is it?" Buffy replied. "Don't you think she puts a damper on fun? Like a three-hundred-foot misprinted flannel blanket that clashes with everything?"

"No, I don't," said Dr. Spinner firmly.

Buffy shot her a look, eyebrows raised.

"Well . . . I can agree that Samantha isn't *always* the most cheerful person," said Dr. Spinner.

Buffy raised her eyebrows even higher.

"Your sister is just fine when she isn't power moping," said her mother.

Buffy walked across the lobby and headed toward the living room.

"I've reserved the front row at my play tonight," she called over her shoulder. "Crews have been working overtime to rebuild the sets. *Scarlett Hydrangea's Secret of the Nile* is even better without clowns throwing pies and rubber pancakes."

Buffy kept talking as she led her mother and aunt into the living room.

"We'll get diamond pedicures during the intermission, and . . ."

Suddenly she became wistful. She turned to one of the room's floor-to-ceiling windows and gazed out over the city.

"There are rainbow unicorns out there somewhere," she said softly.

"I hate to interrupt you," Dr. Spinner said, "but I have a question. It's important."

"Important?" Buffy shot back. "Nothing's more important than unicorns."

She walked to the piano and turned over the sparkly sheet music.

"From here on in, the focus is on the fabulous!" Buffy shouted. "We'll get Broadway-star haircuts and shop for shoes that match our—"

"Buffy," Dr. Spinner interrupted. "How do you ever find time to finish your schoolwork with all this fabulousness?"

Buffy opened her mouth to answer. Then she closed it.

"Her school had to shut down for the semester," said Penny. "Didn't you hear?"

"No, no, no," said Buffy, waving at her aunt. "I didn't want to bother her with that."

"What happened exactly?" asked Dr. Spinner, raising one eyebrow suspiciously.

"Apparently, there was so much rain in California that they canceled school," said Penny.

The color in Dr. Spinner's cheeks started to change to bubble-gum pink.

"At . . . least . . . ," Penny continued slowly, "that's what Buffy told . . . me . . . and . . ."

"Hollywood isn't like Seattle, Mother," Buffy said very quickly. "They have to watch out for the rain there. I just came here for a weekend. But when I heard there might be a storm in California, it didn't make sense to travel all the way back to see if the weather changed."

Dr. Spinner's face turned beet red. She reached into her pocket and took out her phone.

"Now, wait, Mother," said Buffy, watching her dial. "You don't have to use your phone."

Nervously, she looked back and forth between her aunt and mother.

"I'm getting a complete education right here," Buffy said faster than before. "I'm studying art and high fashion. I'm learning the biology of unicorns—and the physics of shoe storage."

Buffy raced across the living room and picked up her ibis scepter from the coffee table.

"And let's not forget about my play," she continued, waving the scepter. "I'm majoring in historical drama and licensed theater criticism. Not to mention mermaid wrangling, and all that marketing and promotion and . . ."

Dr. Spinner pointed two fingers at Buffy and made eye contact. She used her veterinarian stare at full power. It could have stopped 144 chinchillas in their tracks. Buffy froze.

"Hello," her mom said into her phone. "Is this the theater?"

Buffy stayed frozen.

"This is Scarlett Hydrangea's mother," she said sternly. "Tell everyone to go home. The play is closed. Permanently."

CHAPTER SEVEN

ONE WAY OR ANOTHER

Samantha gazed up and down Central Park West. The street swarmed with cars, buses, delivery trucks, and cabs. She'd walked all the way from Buffy's apartment with Uncle Paul in silence, his flip-flops slapping against the pavement. Gradually he seemed to have regained a little bounce in his step, though Samantha didn't want to ask him any more questions just yet. The message from her father seemed to have seriously affected him, although she had no idea why.

She watched as her uncle stepped forward and raised one hand in the air. He looked like he was going to wave at an approaching taxi. Then he put his hand down. He put the tips of both index fingers to his lips as if he was about to whistle. Then he stopped himself.

He was a master of super-secret travel, but he clearly was having trouble with regular travel just now.

Samantha smiled.

She bent down and rested the trombone case on the sidewalk. Then she flipped the latches and opened it. She pulled out the umbrella and began to wave it at the traffic.

"Taxi!" she called. "Taxi, taxi!"

Suddenly her uncle was rushing over to her.

"Waitaminute, waitaminute!" he said. "Put that away."

Samantha stopped waving the umbrella.

"I'll cancel the plane tickets," said Uncle Paul. "Then . . . PSST!"

"PSST!" she repeated cheerfully as she stowed the umbrella back in the trombone case.

"Thanks, Samantha," he added. "I guess I was so distracted thinking about those *clogs* that I forgot about super secrets for a minute."

Samantha still wasn't sure what that was all about, but it was good to have Uncle Paul back again.

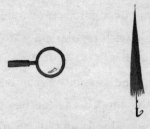

CHAPTER EIGHT

TRY A NEW ANGLE

Samantha and her uncle walked out of the Christopher Street subway station at Seventh Avenue.

"Do you want to stop for ice cream?" said Uncle Paul, looking around. "I know a few good places very close by."

"Really?" Samantha asked, confused. "Is that why we're here? Ice cream?"

"I guess it's hasty ways versus tasty days," he said.

She couldn't tell if her uncle was telling her something important or just having fun.

"Do you want me to record that in my journal?" she asked.

"Nah," he said. "But I really do like ice cream."

Samantha shrugged.

"But here's something you might want to write down for the future," he added.

Samantha waited.

"Titanic . . . Dynamite . . . Library," said Uncle Paul.

Before she could ask him what he meant, he was walking away along Seventh Avenue. Her uncle had returned to normal. Of course, it was Uncle Paul normal. That always included mysteries and puzzles. She followed after him.

"Stop," he said suddenly. "Look down."

A triangle-shaped plaque about two feet long on each side lay embedded in the sidewalk surrounded by cement. On it, black tiles formed letters against a white-tile background.

"Property of the Hess Estate," Samantha read, squinting to make out the words. "Which has never been dedicated for public purposes."

"That's not the important part," said Uncle Paul. "Watch this."

He knelt and waved his index finger over a row of three small white tiles inside the triangle.

"Tie . . . die . . . lie," he said, and tapped the small tile on the right.

Then he stood up and brushed some dirt from his knee.

"That's it," said Uncle Paul.

Samantha looked around. Cars and busses whizzed by on the street. A steady stream of people pushed past them on the sidewalk in both directions.

"What do you mean, that's it?" she asked. "What's *tie . . . die . . . lie?*"

"That's how I remember the three settings on the triangle. Titanic . . . Dynamite . . . Library," said Uncle Paul. "It was aimed at the wreck of the RMS *Titanic*. Now it's aimed at Dynamite."

"Dynamite," she repeated. "The magtrain station, right?"

He nodded and started to walk, waving for her to follow.

"Come on," said Uncle Paul. "I'll explain when we're on the slingshot trolley."

Samantha followed him, swinging the trombone case as she went. He led her back into the subway station, down the stairs, and through the turnstile. The platform was swarming with people waiting for the next uptown train.

"I thought you said slingshot trolley," she said. "Is that your secret name for the subway?"

"No," he replied. "We're just taking the subway back to Central Park."

The train was approaching, so they squeezed themselves into the crowd and waited for it to pull into the station.

"To Cleopatra's Needle," Uncle Paul said.

The train rumbled to a stop, the doors opened, and Samantha followed him into the tightly packed front car. As Samantha stood wedged between two passengers, she counted nine shopping bags between them. It made her think of Aunt Penny.

The train rolled and shook. Samantha steadied herself and peeked over the shopping bags at her uncle. He smiled to himself as he studied a framed subway map on the train wall. The train rocked, and she leaned on her trombone case, holding it tightly.

Through a dozen legs on the crowded train, her uncle's new orange flip-flops gleamed brightly.

They would go to Cleopatra's Needle and find a slingshot trolley. Then . . . maybe . . . she was going to learn *everything*.

CHAPTER NINE

UNDER STATEMENT

Samantha followed her uncle through Central Park and walked up the same staircase she had climbed with Nipper over a month ago. In the center of a redbrick terrace, a huge stone obelisk emerged from a square granite base.

"Cleopatra's Needle," said Samantha. "I was here with Nipper last month."

Uncle Paul nodded. He hopped over the metal railing that surrounded the monument.

"Climb over, and let's get this thing moving," he said.

She gazed up at the towering stone monument. Worn carvings of ancient Egyptian symbols covered every surface. She shrugged and placed her trombone case on the other side of the railing. Then she took her uncle's hand. He helped her scale the three-foot-high barrier and hop down. As soon as she landed, he let go and stepped up to the obelisk. He leaned into it, shoving hard with both hands.

"Push with me," said Uncle Paul.

Together they strained and shoved until, suddenly, it budged.

A deep scraping sound rumbled, and the giant obelisk began to turn. At first, it felt very heavy and was difficult to move. After a quarter rotation, it seemed to loosen a bit. It still took some strength, but the obelisk began to move more easily.

"I can't believe it," said Samantha.

"Believe what?" Uncle Paul asked. "That there's a secret entrance? This can't be the most amazing thing you've seen so far."

"No," Samantha replied. "I can't believe *Nipper* was right about moving this monument."

The obelisk rotated as they continued to push a second time around the granite base.

"This is so much harder alone," her uncle said as they pushed. "Here comes three."

Just as they reached the end of the third cycle, two metallic clicks echoed inside the stone base. It sounded like a large, heavy lock opening.

Uncle Paul stopped pushing, so Samantha did, too. He grabbed her suitcase, knelt down, and pushed on

the side of the monument base. It swung inward, like a dog door. He looked back at her.

"See you at the bottom," he said.

Then he winked and disappeared through the swinging door.

Samantha looked around the terrace to make sure she was alone. She slipped her arm through the large handle of her trombone case, turned back to the panel, and pushed her head inside. A dimly lit shaft led straight down below the needle. A ladder on the far wall lined the shaft. Looking down, she could just barely make out the shape of her uncle, working his way down the ladder.

She reached out and grasped a ladder rung with her free hand, stepped out with one foot, and let her trombone case hang from her arm.

Slowly and somewhat awkwardly, she started to climb down.

"I made it," her uncle called from somewhere beneath her. "Sixty-nine feet under the park."

Samantha remembered that Cleopatra's Needle rose sixty-nine feet above the ground. She didn't get many chances to look down as she descended, however. During most of the climb, she kept her eyes on her hands—and her hands on the ladder. It would be good to get home so she could ditch the trombone case. Traveling with the umbrella was easy—when you could just sling it over your shoulder.

After a while, the space around her grew brighter. Samantha stopped to check out her surroundings. The shaft had widened as she'd climbed down. Below her was an empty chamber with one open exit. She only had a few feet to go, so she climbed down three more rungs and then hopped onto the floor, landing hard on cement. The trombone case slid down her arm, but she grabbed the handle before she dropped it. It took a few seconds to regain her balance.

Uncle Paul wasn't there.

"Hello?" she said.

Her voice echoed back up the shaft.

"Over here," Uncle Paul called. "I'm at the slingshot trolley."

Samantha followed her uncle's voice through the exit and into a hallway where he was standing in another chamber beside a shiny silver vehicle. She guessed it was about twice as long as a car. It came to a long point in the front. A clear canopy rested on a hinge at an angle, revealing a two-person cockpit. Fins stuck out the back. To Samantha, it looked like a fighter jet without wings.

"So that's the slingshot trolley," she said.

"Yes. That's what they call it," said her uncle. "I know you're much better at making up names for things like this."

"Actually, yes," said Samantha. "On the way to Machu Picchu, I made up dozens of names for the terrace train, or the balcony buggy, or— Wait. Who's *they*?"

She hoped to get some actual information now, but Uncle Paul had already climbed up and over the side of the strange vehicle. He sat inside the cockpit with her suitcase on his lap and waved for her to join him.

Samantha grabbed the edge of the opening with both hands and pulled herself over the side. She landed on a padded leather bench next to her uncle.

His hand hovered over a bright red button on the dashboard in front of them.

"Buckle up," he told her. "You'll like this."

Samantha looked down and saw two parts of an X-shaped harness. It was just like the restraint on the terrible rocket ride from Mali to Indonesia—when Nipper launched the hydro rocket before she had a chance to "buckle up." She put the trombone case on the floor between her feet and snapped the two parts of the harness together quickly.

"Hang on," said Uncle Paul. "I've done this a hundred times, and it's still always a bit of a jolt."

He slapped the button.

Hiss. Hiss. Hiss. Hiss.

The vehicle slid backward a few feet and then again three more times.

Uncle Paul slapped the button again.

A hurricane of steam swirled around the vehicle and . . .

SHOOM!

Samantha sank back into her chair as they shot forward. The walls of the tunnel blurred, and she felt pressure on her eyelids. It was hard to blink. She could barely move. The force of the acceleration kept her pressed tight against the back of the seat. Her arms stayed stuck at her sides. But she was fine with that. Happily, unlike that time on the hydro rocket, she felt prepared for this ride. Also, she wasn't upside down, shoeless, and sopping wet.

"I bet this is what it's like to take off from an aircraft carrier," Uncle Paul said over the sound of the vibrating, speeding craft.

Samantha eyed one of the metal fasteners holding the cockpit together. It reminded her of the rivets on the Eiffel Tower. Did the same people design these things? She really needed to find some way to get her uncle to tell her everything.

"So, who built this . . . trolley?" she asked casually.

"Same folks who built the magtrain," Uncle Paul answered.

"And who were *they*?" she asked.

"Well," said Uncle Paul, "the same folks who—"

"And who were *they*?" Samantha interrupted, a little louder.

"Ah yes," said Uncle Paul, gazing around the cockpit.

He looked right at her with a serious expression.

"We've got almost an hour until we reach Dynamite," he said. "Let's start . . . almost at the beginning this time."

Samantha tried not to show her excitement. She waited, hoping that this was finally *it*, the moment when she would learn *everything*.

"There's a magtrain station at Dynamite, Washington," he said.

"Oh, I know that," said Samantha. "I want to know who built it."

Uncle Paul smiled and nodded.

"Yes, I'll start by giving you a WEATHER report," he said.

Samantha smiled. "And the slidewalks," she said. "I want to know all the places they go."

"Of course," said Uncle Paul.

"And what's up with dog clogs?" she added.

Uncle Paul stopped smiling.

Samantha immediately regretted her words. Her uncle was staring off into space again. He began to rub his forehead. She had no idea what he was thinking.

Lights pulsed overhead as they rocketed through the tunnel. Samantha glanced around the cab and noticed a small compartment behind them. Several shiny rectangular objects rested on the floor.

"Are those gold bars?" she asked.

"Maybe," said Uncle Paul. "Wait. I'm sorry. What did you say?"

Samantha didn't ask again.

She had lost him to the dog clogs for the second time that day. Would he recover before they reached home?

The slingshot trolley hurtled onward.

Samantha thought about Nipper, somewhere in Seattle. She would help her dad find her brother. Then maybe she'd spend a little time on her own life—the not-so-super-secret parts that included summer and friends.

Okay, maybe not so many friends, she told herself. In the past few months, she'd spent so much time racing around the world with her brother, defeating the RAIN and the SUN, she hadn't had much time for friends. She didn't even have many sort-of, kind-of friends out there.

"Dog clogs," Uncle Paul said again.

Samantha decided that as soon as she saved Nipper, she'd definitely make some new friends.

Sort of, kind of.

The Hess Triangle

A tile triangle, about two feet on each side, is built into the sidewalk at the corner of Christopher Street and Seventh Avenue South in New York City, New York.

In 1910, the family of David Hess owned a five-story apartment building. The city of New York forced him to sell his building to make room for the new subway system. The city made a mistake, however, and left the Hess family with a small triangle-shaped patch of land. A plaque remains on that spot to this day, declaring that it is "property of the Hess Estate which has never been dedicated for public purposes."

At 0.0000797113 of an acre, the Hess Triangle is the smallest privately owned piece of real estate in New York City.

Thousands of New Yorkers walk over the triangle every day without noticing it. Or taking a closer look.

* * *

A three-way switch beneath the Hess Triangle is the secret control for the ultra-high-speed "slingshot trolley" stationed beneath Cleopatra's Needle in Central Park.

Tapping one of three special tiles will point the vehicle toward the Library of Congress, the wreck of the RMS *Titanic*, or an empty field in Dynamite, a suburb of Spokane, Washington.

CHAPTER TEN

UNEXPLAINED VANISHING BROTHER

Samantha and Uncle Paul entered through the side door.

"Wruf!" barked Dennis.

The pug's plastic cone clattered on the kitchen floor as he scampered up to them.

Samantha thought he was going to lick her hand, the way he usually greeted people. Instead, he darted behind her uncle, as if hiding from something.

"I am one hundred percent glad to see both of you two," said her father.

George Spinner wore a headband with a glowing lamp on the front, about the size and shape of a quarter. It was bright, but not as bright as some of the lightbulbs he often brought home from work at the

American Institute of Lamps. He sat at the kitchen table, surrounded by charts, maps, a pad of graph paper, and his professional set of 256 colored markers. An unidentifiable electric gadget blinked in one of his hands.

Samantha decided that it really was a good thing she and her uncle had come back from New York to help. Her dad was a genius with electronics and math, but she doubted he could find Nipper if he were in the next room.

Samantha heard a tapping sound. She looked at Dennis. The pug pawed at his cone. His claws rattled on the plastic.

"When you take care of your loved ones, sometimes you have to do things that seem ridiculous," said Uncle Paul.

Samantha wasn't sure if he was talking about the dog's cone, her father's gadgets, or maybe something else. He had relaxed and switched back to normal during their ride home, but she didn't ask him any more questions for the rest of the trip. She didn't want to set him off again.

Bzzt. Zzt-zzt.

Her uncle froze. His eyes shifted left and right. Something had set him off again.

Bzzt. Zzt-zzt.

The sound was coming from . . . Samantha looked down. Her dad wore blue shoes she had never seen before.

Bzzt. Zzt-zzt.

And they buzzed.

They looked, just a little, like traditional Dutch wooden shoes: clogs. She had learned about them years ago when her class studied the Netherlands. But these were made of blue plastic and had tiny lightbulbs pointing forward. Wires and miniature electronic parts clung to the sides and top. Each shoe had a small video panel above the heel. Samantha suspected these were the "dog clogs."

Bzzt. Zzt-zzt.

The shoes buzzed again. Uncle Paul shook his head, as if he were trying to clear out marbles that were rolling around in his brain.

"Why, George?" he asked Samantha's dad. "We're missing a kid, not a dog."

"I've adjusted the frequency," said Mr. Spinner. "They should be able to pick up the sounds of any coins or toys or other items if they fall out of Nipper's pockets."

He looked at Samantha.

"That sort of thing happens a lot, you know," he said.

She nodded.

Samantha watched as her father stood up, reached down with a tiny screwdriver, and tapped at one of the clogs.

"Really, Dad?" asked Samantha. "Electronic shoes?"

"Electricity and magnetism can produce all kinds of interesting effects," said her father, turning a small screw in both directions.

"You're not kidding," said Uncle Paul, pulling at one of his ears.

The sound from the dog clogs seemed to really bother him. Samantha didn't like the buzzing sound, either, but it wasn't as bad as Uncle Paul made it seem. As she watched him, he tugged at his ear two more times.

"Are these shoes really helping you find Nipper, Dad?" she asked.

"Well . . . I haven't had any luck so far," he said, and twisted another small screw back and forth.

Her father stood up, turned, and grabbed something from the table. It was Nipper's hand lens. Her father closed one eye and stared at her through the glass.

"Maybe the clues are already here and I just don't know where to look," he said.

The beam of his headlamp glowed through the magnifier toward Samantha's face, forcing her to squint.

"Can I hold the hand lens for now?" asked Samantha.

Her dad looked confused.

"That's what some people call a magnifying glass," she added.

"Oh. Of course," said Mr. Spinner, passing it to her.

Samantha dropped the lens into her purse. If she was going to use the Plans to help find Nipper, she'd need it for sure.

"I've been racking my brain," said Mr. Spinner. "Maybe someone other than Nipper himself is responsible for his disappearance."

He walked over to the table, picked up a notepad, and tapped at it.

"Is there anyone in our neighborhood who has a history of making threats or saying aggressive and violent things to Nipper?" he asked.

Samantha smiled. She could think of someone.

"The tiniest detail could be a clue," said Mr. Spinner. "Maybe there's someone who addresses him by his full name instead of the nickname we all use."

Samantha smiled a little more. Someone definitely came to mind.

"Okay, Dad," she said. "Take off that headlamp."

She waited for him to remove the light. Then she headed across the room.

"Follow me," she said, and opened the side door.

CHAPTER ELEVEN

ON A ROLL

"Nowhere! Nowhere!"

The parrot squawked as the yarn ball rocked.

Inside, Nipper shifted his weight. The ball started rocking faster and faster. Suddenly it jerked to a stop.

"I thought I told you not to move," Missy growled.

Through a gap in the mustard-yellow yarn, Nipper saw Missy's shadow. He felt her breath close to his ear.

"I don't enjoy trapping and starving people," she told him. "Well, maybe I do. But that's not the point."

"Oh, come on, Missy," said Nipper. "I don't know how much more of this I can take. Could you at least make the parrot go away?"

"Aweigh! Aweigh!"

"Sammy can go wherever she wants," growled Missy. "But *you* are staying here until I can get my hands on . . . Hold on."

He heard her walk away, and then there was silence. Nipper wondered if he was alone.

Suddenly Missy's face popped up in front of his. Between the strands of yarn, she stared directly at him.

Nipper gasped. It was terrifying.

Then he heard more voices in the distance.

"Listen, you," she growled. "I have to take care of something. Don't go anywhere."

"*Anywhere!*" the bird squawked.

Nipper heard Missy stomp up the porch steps and the screen door slam as she went back into her house.

He waited a minute and then started swaying as hard as he could. The ball rocked and rocked until it finally turned over and he started to roll. Head over heels, he moved across the driveway, away from the house.

"*Don't go! Don't go!*" screeched the bird. "*Don't go! Don't—*"

Crunch!

The ball shook around him. He figured he must have just rolled through the bushes between the Snoddgrass house and his own. He tried to stop, but he couldn't. He was pretty sure he rolled past the basketball hoop on his own driveway. Then the ball gained speed.

"*Go!*" the bird squawked in the distance.

Crash!

The ball shook, and the sound of splintering wood faded as he rolled. He was rolling and tumbling faster and faster. He couldn't hear the parrot anymore.

Over and over he went.

Smack! Bump!

The ball crashed into something, and he bounced. He felt an object fly out of his pocket. He had no way to know where he was or what was going on outside the ball. Itchy mustard-yellow yarn rubbed against his face.

He heard the sounds of cars and buses growing louder. He closed his eyes . . . and rolled. Not that he had a choice.

CHAPTER TWELVE

THE DRIVE WAY

Samantha led her father and uncle to the Snoddgrass house.

"I've already been here five times," said Mr. Spinner. "I even rang the doorbell *nineteen* times."

"This way," Samantha said, directing them to the driveway. "Whenever Nipper comes over, he heads here."

As soon as they turned away from the porch, Missy burst from the front door and waved to them.

"Good afternoon, George and Samantha," she called.

Missy pointed in Uncle Paul's direction.

"You too, weirdly dressed stranger whom I've never, ever seen before," she said.

Uncle Paul smiled and nodded at her.

0100300004001000

The girl who lived next door always seemed strange to Samantha. Now she was acting extra strange. Almost like she was nervous. She kept looking over at Uncle Paul.

"Samantha suggested we explore your driveway for signs of Nipper," Mr. Spinner called.

"You can't," Missy snapped. "I mean . . . please wait until later. My pet parrot is taking a nap right now, and it would be rude to disturb her."

"Sammy?" asked Samantha.

"Yes," said Missy. "Sammy the parrot is my discomfort pet."

"Discomfort pet?" asked Samantha. "We need to go down there and make sure—"

"Okay," her father interrupted. "Let us know when it's a good time to come back and investigate."

"Hold on, Dad," said Samantha, raising her hand and turning to face Missy. "If there are any clues about Nipper down there, we don't want to wait just so your bird can nap."

"Clues?" Missy replied.

She glared at Samantha for a few seconds. Then, suddenly, she stood up straight and called to Samantha's father.

"I just remembered," she said cheerfully. "My parents wanted to tell you something about young Jeremy."

Before Samantha could say anything else, Missy scurried back into her house, letting the screen door swing shut behind her. There was the sound of foot-steps going upstairs, followed by footsteps stomping back down.

"Hello again, Spinners," Missy called.

A man and a woman stood behind Missy Snoddgrass, one on each side. They were framed perfectly by the screen. They were both very neatly dressed and wore big smiles on their faces.

Samantha was sure that she'd never seen them be-fore. She definitely would have remembered these two. The man held up a coffee mug displaying the words *World's Greatest Dad*, and the woman pointed to a blue ribbon pinned to her chest. The words *PTA Mom of the Year* sparkled in glittery letters.

"You know my parents, George," said Missy.

"I don't think so," he replied, eyeing the people be-hind her. He looked just as confused as Samantha felt.

"Well, my mom and dad know all about *you*," said Missy.

The woman winked at Samantha's father. She flashed a smile at Samantha. Then, still smiling, she nodded several times at Uncle Paul.

Samantha wondered if those were really Missy's par-ents. How many weird people lived in that house? She didn't really want to find out.

"My parents told me they saw a boy heading to Vol-unteer Park an hour ago," said Missy.

The couple behind her began to nod enthusiastically.

Samantha was already suspicious about Missy's story. The two weird nodding adults only made her more so.

"How do you know it was Nipper?" she asked.

The couple stopped smiling and nodding. They turned to look at Missy, as if waiting to find out, too.

"He was very annoying," said Missy. "And he was touching and poking at things and not paying attention. And he wouldn't stop talking about the New York Yankees."

The couple started smiling and nodding in agreement again.

"That sounds like Nipper," said Samantha's father.

Samantha looked over at Uncle Paul to see if he thought this whole scene was strange, too. He was busy tugging at his ears. The dog clogs must have been bothering him again.

"So," Missy said, pointing to the park at the end of the block. "You really should head in that direction and see if anyone knows anything about anything."

"We still need to check your driveway," said Samantha.

"Samantha's right," Uncle Paul told Missy, dropping his hands to his sides. "We should have a look around just in case."

"I already told you," Missy snapped. "You can't wake the bird!"

Samantha noticed that Missy's hands were balled tightly into fists.

"Isn't that right, *Mother* and *Father*?"

The people behind her started nodding again in unison.

"Have you searched your own driveway yet?" Missy asked.

"Not thoroughly," Samantha's father answered.

"Then you should *thoroughly* go away and leave us alone until you do!" she barked, and slammed the heavy inside door.

The Spinners stood on the Snoddgrass porch for a moment, stunned.

"Don't go! Don't go! Don't go! Don't go!"

A high-pitched voice squawked from far off.

"Enough of this foolishness," said Samantha, turning toward the side of the house.

"I don't remember meeting those parents before," said Samantha's dad.

"And there's something really familiar about that girl," said Uncle Paul. "I just can't remember where I've seen her before."

Bzzt! Zzzzzzzzzzzt!

Mr. Spinner's shoes buzzed, much louder than before.

"Ugh," said Uncle Paul, closing one eye and tilting his head.

Bzzt! Zzzzzzzzzzzt!

"Quick, everyone," Samantha's father said excitedly. "Look at my heels!"

"You sound just like Buffy," said Uncle Paul, pressing his hands over his ears.

Samantha watched her uncle. The sound really did bother him. She bent down and looked at her father's dog clogs. The small video panels on each heel flashed the same word:

_ S _ P _ O _ O _ N _

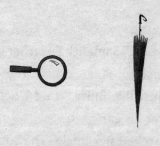

CHAPTER FOURTEEN

THE HOLE TRUTH

"Spoon?" asked Samantha.

"I told you," said her father. "I tuned my clogs to detect objects falling out of pockets."

Samantha rolled her eyes and looked to her uncle for help. To her surprise, he nodded at both of them.

"I did give Nipper a mustache spoon last winter," said Uncle Paul.

"A mustache spoon?" asked Samantha. "What's that?"

"They used to be popular," he said.

"The boy can't be more than a mile away," said Samantha's dad. "Even modern electronics have limits."

Mr. Spinner stepped down from the Snoddgrass porch and began to look up and down Thirteenth Avenue. He squinted at the water tower far off in the park. Then he turned to face the other direction.

"I think we should go back to our house," he said. "I'll start making a map of places to investigate. Maybe we make a list of playgrounds or places that sell New York Yankees merchandise."

"Didn't Buffy call you with my list?" asked Samantha.

"List?" he asked.

Samantha grunted. Her dad clearly had no idea what she was talking about. She wasn't really surprised that Buffy didn't bother to get him her list. Maybe if she had used gold ink and written it on the side of a shoe . . .

"Follow me," she said, and began leading her dad and uncle up the driveway.

"Let's look behind our house first," said Mr. Spinner, stopping and pointing sideways to their backyard.

"Sure," said Uncle Paul. "Maybe take the shoes off for a while, too."

Samantha was starting to feel as if she was the only person in the world capable of paying attention to anything for more than three seconds.

"Is anyone serious about finding Nipper at all?" Samantha asked.

"We are," her father and Uncle Paul said at the same time.

Samantha turned. They were both pointing sideways.

The bushes between the two houses were crushed flat. A trail of flattened twigs and grass continued off toward the Spinners' house.

"See?" said her father. "There's a hole in our back fence."

Samantha looked over at their fence, and sure enough, in the distance, past the garage, at the far end of her own backyard, there was a hole in the fence. The fence was fine when she'd left for New York last week.

"We'll find that boy soon," said Mr. Spinner.

Samantha noticed that her father sounded confident for a change. She watched him step over the flattened bushes and head into their yard, shoes buzzing as he went. She took one more glance down the Snoddgrass driveway. Then she followed.

As soon as she cleared the bushes, she looked back. Uncle Paul was coming, too, but he walked at a much slower pace. Samantha guessed he was allowing a few extra yards between him and her father's buzzing shoes.

CHAPTER FIFTEEN

THE BOY IN THE BALL

Nipper rolled and rolled. He had no idea where he was heading, but he was definitely going downhill fast.

Bump!

His ball slammed into something solid, and he banked sideways. Did he hit a parked car? A mailbox? It might have been an elephant, for that matter. He couldn't see much beyond the yellow yarn.

Nipper felt something else sliding from his pocket, but he couldn't move his head to check on it. He tried to reach with his hand, and the yarn gave a little. His fingertip brushed against a metal object. He could feel small sharp bumps, and it felt as if it might be engraved. Then it slipped away.

Clink! Crunch!

Had he lost his really fancy watch?

Nipper kept rolling, but the ball was slowing down. He moved his hand. The yarn around him had loosened a bit. Two more turns and he could move his whole arm. He turned and turned and turned, and with every rotation he unwound until he finally came to a stop.

He was so dizzy! He waited for the universe to stop spinning.

"That's one way to escape from Missy," he said, clawing his way through the rest of the ball. Slowly he emerged from the yarn.

He rose to his feet and saw . . . an elephant!

Nipper smiled at the Elephant Car Wash sign. Everyone smiles when they see the two-story pink neon sign shaped like an elephant. Still smiling, he watched it rotate for a while. Then he turned around and tried to retrace his path. He must have rolled down Capitol Hill, turned, continued four blocks south, and stopped here at the car wash.

Something on the wall caught his eye: a shiny badge, about the size and shape of a quarter, sparkled at eye level a few feet away. He leaned in and took a closer look. It was a small white circle with an icon of a person in the center:

"How many other people get stuck in giant balls of yarn?" he asked.

An SUV drove into the car wash, and the sound of water spraying and spinning mops brushing against metal and glass made Nipper think about slurping a milkshake. He really could use a snack.

He tapped the little badge.

Whoosh!

A blast of water shoved him sideways.

"Waitaminute!" he spluttered.

He flailed his arms and tried to regain his balance, but he slipped on wet yarn.

"Waitaminute!" he shouted again.

An opening had appeared in the side of the building.

Whoosh!

A second watery blast forced Nipper forward. Head over heels, he tumbled through the opening.

He skidded into darkness, soaked, surprised, and speckled with stray strands of yarn.

CHAPTER SIXTEEN

STORMY WEATHER

Samantha stood with her father and uncle at the far end of their backyard, studying the huge round hole in the fence.

"A giant ball did that," said her father.

"Creative," said her uncle. "Suzette asked you not to play ball *in* the house."

"No, no," said her father. "This happened without me."

He ran his hand over the splintered wood.

"I think this was done only a short time ago," he added.

Samantha looked through the hole and into the alley beyond. A few yards farther, the street led across Capitol Hill and then downtown.

"Come on," she said, glancing back at them. "Let's catch up with Nipper."

One by one, they stepped through the broken fence and walked along the alley. Her father led the way, and Samantha kept pace a few feet behind. Uncle Paul brought up the rear.

The dog clogs had stopped buzzing, but Samantha could tell her uncle was still bothered. Was it just the memory of the sound? Or was it something else?

Ten minutes later, they were halfway down the hill.

"Ah, Space Needle," her father said, gazing off into the distance. "You'll shine just fine tonight. No more potentiometer trouble for you."

He walked on, mumbling about how to convert candlepower to lumens.

Uncle Paul tapped Samantha on the shoulder and signaled to let her father walk ahead of them.

"Watch out," he said, leaning in close to her.

Samantha noticed that her uncle looked very serious suddenly.

"Watch out," he repeated, adding, "for the CLOUD."

"Really?" she asked. "Since when?"

In New York, her uncle had warned Nipper to watch out for the WIND. This was something new.

"Since we headed into this part of town," he answered.

"So I don't have to watch out for the WIND?" she asked.

"You'll definitely have to do that in the long run," said Uncle Paul. "But right now and right here, you'll have to watch out for the CLOUD."

"Who are they?" asked Samantha, eager for any information at all.

"I don't know a lot about them," he replied. "We never really worried about them until recently."

"Recently?" she asked.

"It's definitely going to be important to you soon," he said, nodding.

"Wait," said Samantha. "Who's *them* and who's *we*? And . . . what was *it*?"

She was getting really confused.

"I guess that was a lot of pronouns," said Uncle Paul.

He scratched his ear and looked ahead to her father.

"They make it hard for me to think," he said.

He looked back at Samantha again.

"By *they*, I meant the dog clogs," he added.

"Fine," said Samantha, giving up a little.

She was totally pronoun-ed out.

They had reached the bottom of the hill. Traffic zoomed by on the street. A few blocks away, the saucer-shaped top of the Space Needle seemed to float in the sky.

"Come on, you two!" her father called.

"You know, Samantha," Uncle Paul said quickly. "There are many super secrets that aren't on that umbrella."

Samantha glanced at the umbrella over her shoulder and then ahead to where her father had stopped, waiting for them to catch up.

"Remember," said Uncle Paul, speaking faster. "When you go all the way down, watch out for the CLOUD."

"Down?" she asked. "You mean downtown?"

"My shoes seem to have lost the signal!" Mr. Spinner called.

Samantha glanced ahead to her father and back to her uncle.

"Aren't you worried that *he* is going to hear some of this?" she whispered.

"Not really," said Uncle Paul. "Go ahead. Try it."

They reached Mr. Spinner and stopped in front of him.

"Hello," he said.

Samantha opened her purse, took out her purple octagon sunglasses, and put them on. She also took out Nipper's hand lens. Then she raised her umbrella over her head and popped it open.

"Dad," she said. "Notice anything strange or mysterious?"

"Let's see . . . ," he replied, rubbing his chin thoughtfully.

Mr. Spinner stared at her sunglasses and at the magnifying glass. From there, he looked up at her umbrella.

He squinted at the lining. Then he gazed past it to the Space Needle hovering in the sky a few blocks away.

"I wonder how that lightbulb broke on the Space Needle last night," he said. "That is definitely mysterious."

"See what I mean?" said Uncle Paul.

Samantha agreed. Her father's thoughts were elsewhere. She closed her umbrella and slung it over her shoulder. While she put the glasses and hand lens back in her purse, something on the sidewalk caught her eye. A long strand of mustard-yellow yarn. She followed it with her eyes and realized it formed a trail. It curved to the left and continued south for several blocks in the direction of the Elephant Car Wash. She could see the big pink sign rotating in the distance and smiled. That sign always made her smile. She pointed for Uncle Paul to look, too.

To her surprise, when her uncle spotted the pink elephant-shaped sign, he didn't smile. Instead, he looked thoughtful.

"Look what I just found," announced her father.

Samantha and Uncle Paul both turned to see that he was holding up a thin, curved piece of shiny metal.

"It's a boomerang," he said. "And it seems to be made of steel."

He handed the object to Samantha. It definitely looked like a boomerang. Her third-grade class had studied Australia. Boomerangs were originally used for hunting there. Today, they are mostly used for sport. She'd never heard of one made out of metal, though.

"Boomerangs let you play catch without friends," said her father.

Uncle Paul leaned close to her.

"There are also times when you really need friends, Samantha," he whispered in her ear. "And I can't . . ."

Bzzt! Zzzzzzzzzzzt!

"Car!" her father shouted. He was looking down at the back of his shoe. "Somebody dropped a car!"

"That's it," said Uncle Paul. "We have to go home."

He turned to Samantha's father.

"Come on, George," he said. "I have a new theory about finding Nipper."

"Theories are good," said her father.

Before Samantha could protest, the two men started back up the hill.

She looked at the Elephant Car Wash sign again. She didn't smile this time. Samantha looked at the boomerang, then followed her father and her uncle.

"Did you decide that our neighbors are correct?" she heard her father ask Uncle Paul. "Do you think Nipper could have headed to Volunteer Park?"

"It's possible," said Uncle Paul, leading the way now.

As they walked back up the hill, Samantha heard the dog clogs buzz several more times. The sound wasn't so bad, but each time it rang out, Uncle Paul shook his head dramatically.

"How does someone drop a car?" she heard her father wonder out loud.

Samantha decided that if her uncle was so-mysterious and she was so-serious, then her father was definitely *so-ridiculous*!

She kept following . . . and kept wondering about the CLOUD, the WIND, and if it was going to be up to her to find Nipper all by herself.

CHAPTER SEVENTEEN

BOYS AND GIRLS

"Smell the sock . . . find the boy!" said Samantha's father.

Samantha stood in the kitchen, watching her father dangle Nipper's tube sock in front of Dennis's face.

"Smell the sock . . . find the boy!" he repeated.

"Wruf!" the little dog barked.

"I don't think he has any idea what you're doing," said Samantha.

She glanced behind her. Uncle Paul stood by the waffle iron, cooking away. A dozen plates sat along the counter, piled high with fresh hot waffles. He stirred his fifth batch of batter.

"Smell the sock . . ." Her father's voice trailed off.

Dennis turned away from him and stared up at the counter.

"Can you stop breakfast-making for a few minutes?" Mr. Spinner said to Uncle Paul. "I'm trying to establish Nipper's odor."

"Nipper doesn't need any help with that," Uncle Paul called over his shoulder.

Samantha giggled. She watched her uncle at his waffle iron. She knew he was a waffle fan, but this was bonkers! As soon as she announced she wanted to head

back downtown instead of going with them to the park, he started griddling. He had pulled every cookbook from the kitchen cabinets and stacked them in piles between plates on the counter.

"Are you sure you don't want to come to the park with the Spinner boys?" her father asked, still dangling the sock in front of the dog's cone.

"Spinner boys, Dad?" she asked. "You mean you and Uncle Paul?"

"Don't forget Dennis," said her uncle, stirring his batter. "He's a Spinner, too."

"Wruf!" the pug barked when he heard his name.

"Samantha departs, and the search party starts," said her father.

"You know, Samantha," said Uncle Paul as he sprinkled some ingredients into his bowl. "It takes talent to put the right combination of things together."

He started stirring again and looked at her expectantly. He seemed to be waiting for her to figure something out. Samantha still had no idea what to say.

After stirring and staring for a while, Uncle Paul looked at his brother.

"Have you called Suzette yet?" he asked Samantha's father.

"I will . . . ," Mr. Spinner replied, "very soon."

Her father bent down to Dennis and draped the sock over the plastic cone so it hung in front of his face.

"But it would be good to find Nipper first," he added.

"Wruf!" Dennis barked from behind the sock.

"One hundred and forty-four fresh waffles," announced Uncle Paul. "That should be enough for our trip."

He used his waffle tongs to load the steaming disks into a brown paper grocery bag, one by one.

Samantha had had enough of her father's nonsense and her uncle's overboard waffle-making. It was time to get going. She left the three Spinner "boys" behind in the kitchen and paused at the bottom of the stairs to examine the metal object her father discovered on their short trip downtown.

"Boomerang," she said, turning the shiny weapon in her hands.

It was a projectile, but she needed more information. And she knew exactly where to look. She headed up to her bedroom.

Samantha went straight to her desk. She opened the large hardcover book with the words *Encyclopedia Missilium* engraved on the cover. She had borrowed it from Uncle Paul's apartment months ago. It was still in her room from the last time she'd had to identify strange flying objects. Each entry usually included an explanation of a mysterious foe—assuming you knew where to look. She flipped through the pages quickly.

"Here it is," she read. "Straight talk about boomerangs."

She turned several pages until a drawing of a U-shaped object caught her eye. She put her finger on the spot and read:

METAL BOOMERANGS

Boomerangs made of stainless steel are rumored to be a favorite weapon of the Clandestine League of Unstoppable Daredevils, aka the CLOUD. Little is known about this mysterious organization.

It's been rumored that they may have a base beneath downtown Seattle.

See also DIDGERIDOOS, WAGGA WAGGA

"The CLOUD," Samantha repeated. He uncle had mentioned the CLOUD downtown. The daredevils part was new, though.

As usual, the big encyclopedia raised more questions than it answered. She closed the book and headed back downstairs.

In the living room, her father stood by the front door holding something round. Her uncle was waving his hands wildly—not like a great storyteller.

"Please, George," he protested. "Not *another* invention."

"I didn't invent this," Mr. Spinner said. "I got it at the pet expo a few months ago. It's a Blinky Barker. Come here, old pal."

Dennis trotted over to him, and Samantha's father bent down and attached a shiny ring around Dennis's neck, inside the cone.

"Let's go, boys," he said, standing up and opening the door. He stepped outside, and Dennis trotted out of the house after him.

Uncle Paul headed to the door, too. At the last minute, he looked back at Samantha.

"Watch out for the CLOUD," he said again.

"I heard you already," said Samantha. "Any other advice?"

He appeared thoughtful for a moment. Samantha waited.

"Look for the boy in the ball," he said finally.

Then he stepped through the door and caught up with Samantha's father and the pug.

"The boy in the ball?" Samantha repeated to herself.

It didn't seem like useful advice. They'd already guessed that Nipper rolled downtown in some kind of a ball. She sighed. It was one more mysterious statement from the most mysterious man in the world.

Through the living room window, she watched her father and her uncle as they headed down Thirteenth Avenue and disappeared into the park.

Samantha didn't have much confidence that the Spinner *boys* were going to find Nipper. And she wasn't sure she could do it on her own, either. Maybe it was time to find some *girls*.

Of course, thought Samantha, if she had any close friends in her not-so-secret life, they'd be here already. She sighed. It was time to reach out to some sort-of, kind-of friends.

She went back to the kitchen and looked up at the open cabinet. She reached for the only book left after her uncle's breakfast-making blitz: the school directory.

She opened the booklet and flipped the pages until she reached the "H" listings.

"Fiona Hill," she read out loud, writing down a phone number.

Samantha spotted her uncle's empty batter bowl in the sink.

"It takes talent to put the right combination of things together," she said, repeating what her uncle had told her.

Samantha thought about it for a moment. Then she smiled. She needed more than one type of help, and in the right combination.

She went back to the booklet and flipped to the "J" listings.

"Lainey Jain," she said.

CHAPTER EIGHTEEN

MYSTERY DATA

Everyone at school knew about Fiona Hill. She was brilliant.

A lot of people called her "Sherlock Hill." Others called her "Fiona Holmes." Some even called her "Fiona Sherlock Holmes Hill."

"None of those names are particularly creative," Fiona had told Samantha when they met on the school bus last year. "It's a little bit annoying."

Samantha understood all too well. Buffy never stopped calling her "Sammy." And whining about "Sammy." And blaming "Sammy." That was more than a little bit annoying. She made a point of saying "Fiona."

For Samantha, Fiona was a sort-of, kind-of friend. They weren't best buddies, and they never hung out after school. But they said "hi" in class. Also, Samantha had lent her one of her uncle's old-fashioned suitcases to portray Nellie Bly for a history fair. She felt it was okay to ask Fiona for help when she really needed it. And right now, she was exactly the type of friend Samantha really needed: a master detective.

Fiona Hill was known far and wide as the person to turn to when you needed to solve a mystery, answer a puzzle, or track down anything that went missing. She'd won the Lake Union High School Quiz Bowl when she was in the fourth grade. Everybody wanted her on their scavenger hunt teams. Fiona found lost pets, homework, and keys. She helped people recover forgotten passwords.

"Human beings are puzzle pieces," she had told Samantha once. "When you put them together with facts and clues—and each other—you can make a complete picture."

Of course, Samantha knew that little brothers aren't like any other human beings. So she asked Lainey Jain to help, too.

Lainey was brilliant, as well, but she was a specialist. She focused all her intelligence on one topic: kid brothers. She knew how to recognize all their sounds. She could tell you the most popular movies, games, and breakfast cereals for boys between the ages of four and nine. She could explain, in depth, thirteen different types of interruptions.

"Did you know that almost every little brother has a scar somewhere on his head?" she asked as she greeted Samantha and Fiona.

She pointed to her own forehead.

"And almost none of them have any idea how the scar got there," she added.

As soon as they started walking, Lainey dove right in, asking Samantha about Nipper, his friends . . . and all other boys she and Fiona knew, too.

"How about crushes?" she asked loudly over the sound of passing traffic. "Do either of you have a crush?"

Samantha and Fiona looked at each other warily. Neither of them answered.

"I'm just gathering facts," she reassured both of them. "A lot of boys our age have little brothers or *are* little brothers. The more brother-related data we have about Samantha and her world, the easier it will be to find Nipper."

Samantha wasn't sure that was really necessary.

They wound through Capitol Hill for six blocks. Then they turned west on Denny Way and headed downtown.

"I searched near the Elephant Car Wash and found some clues earlier today," Samantha explained as they walked. "I think Nipper disappeared there, but I knew I needed help from people with your special talents."

"Disappeared?" asked Lainey.

Samantha nodded carefully.

"Yes," she answered. "You're going to see that this is a crazy mixed-up situation."

"Have you called your mom?" asked Fiona. "How come you haven't . . . Wait."

She looked at Samantha thoughtfully.

"I suspect your father asked you not to call your mom until he finds Nipper," she concluded.

Samantha nodded.

"Based on that, and on other things you've said, I'm guessing your dad is a little brother, too," Lainey chimed in.

Samantha nodded again.

She smiled to herself as they walked. Quite possibly, she had picked just the right combination of ingredients.

Friends, not ingredients, she reminded herself. Sort of, kind of.

A bus roared by. Samantha raised her voice to make sure Fiona and Lainey could hear her.

"You're about to see stuff that most people miss," said Samantha, "because they don't take a closer look at things."

"That's rarely my problem," said Fiona. "I always pay attention."

As they neared the bottom of the hill, Lainey tapped Samantha on the shoulder.

"I'm still wondering if there is someone special who's caught *your* attention," she insisted. "Someone *you've* taken a closer look at?"

Samantha shook her head. She couldn't think of any boy in Seattle who interested her more than any other. She closed her eyes and tried to picture all the people she'd met in the past few months—ninjas, clowns, super-fruity-slush-bomb vendors. She had no idea if any of them were little brothers. And they certainly weren't crush-worthy.

Somewhere, a motorcycle rumbled above the traffic. It reminded Samantha of her ride through the streets of Mali with the boy named Seydou. She opened her eyes quickly and looked around.

"What about Fiona?" Samantha asked, pointing sideways. "Maybe there's a boy *she* thinks is special?"

"Hey, Fiona," Lainey called quickly. "Is there some special boy you—"

"No," she answered instantly. "Boys are smelly."

Fiona bent down and picked something up from the sidewalk.

"And they break things. No crushes, no thanks," she added, and kept walking.

Lainey turned back to Samantha and winked.

"Here we are," said Samantha, pointing up.

They had arrived at the car wash. Overhead, the big pink elephant sign rotated slowly. The sound of spraying water and spinning brushes drowned out the street traffic.

Samantha saw Lainey smile a little when she spotted the elephant-shaped sign. Then she looked around, confused.

"Is this why we're here?" she asked. "You wanted to show us a car wash?"

"No," said Samantha. "I think there's something really amazing hidden here, and I didn't want to check it out alone."

"Intriguing," said Fiona.

A sports car rumbled up behind them and drove into the car wash.

"Are we going to get wet?" asked Lainey.

"It's not a problem," said Samantha.

She pulled the umbrella from her shoulder and popped it open.

"Careful!" warned Fiona, dodging one of the spokes.

Samantha tilted it to hide the underside from both girls. She definitely didn't want to reveal any super-secret clues about Uncle Paul or the Plans. She needed help finding Nipper, and that was it.

When she saw Fiona bending down to pick something off the sidewalk again, Samantha took her opportunity. She peeked up at the umbrella lining, but without Nipper's hand lens, she couldn't see any details clearly. Samantha closed the umbrella.

"Be on the lookout for anything unusual," she announced.

"How about that?" asked Fiona, pointing to the side of the building.

Samantha followed Fiona's finger and saw a small round marker on the wall:

"The boy in the ball!" said Samantha excitedly.

Uncle *so-mysterious* had actually given her a useful clue!

"The boy in the what?" Lainey asked.

"How do you know it's a boy?" asked Fiona.

"My uncle Paul warned me to watch out for it," she answered.

"Your whole family is kind of mysterious," said Lainey.

"Agreed," said Fiona. "Can you open that umbrella again?"

"Why?" Lainey asked. "Do you think there's something mysterious about Samantha's umbrella, too?"

Samantha looked back and forth between them nervously.

"No," said Fiona, pressing on the little circle. "But an umbrella might be useful. I think this is connected to the—"

Water began to rain down from above, and a section of the wall in front of the girls fell forward, revealing an entrance to a dim hallway. That was when Samantha realized she was sliding into the opening.

"Hang on," she shouted.

"To what exactly?" asked Fiona.

Samantha looked left and right at the smooth walls on either side of her.

"I can't stop!" shouted Lainey.

"Neither can I," called Fiona.

Whoosh! Another blast of water hit them from above. Then, *whoosh!* A wall of water hit them from behind, and the floor fell out from beneath Samantha's feet, and she was coasting down a ramp into the darkness.

CHAPTER NINETEEN

WASHING THE DETECTIVES

Samantha and her companions slid for what she guessed was about as long as two flights of stairs. It was a slippery, barely lit ramp, and everyone kept bumping into the walls and each other.

Near the end of the corridor, the floor leveled out and changed from slippery tile to smooth cement, and one after the other, each girl flopped onto the floor and rolled to a stop.

After a stunned moment, they all started to climb to their feet. As she stood, Samantha noticed the sound of rushing air, and then a motor began to hum. *Is another blast of water coming?* Samantha wondered. She tried to straighten her clothes and hair and pressed on. There was a doorway at the end of the hall.

"This way," she said, pointing her umbrella at the opening.

"What kind of ridiculous and confusing way to travel was that?" asked Lainey, pushing wet hair back from her face.

Samantha thought of the waterslide that she and Nipper rode from Italy to France. She thought about the hydro rocket, the one that had blasted her—upside down and wearing only one shoe—to Indonesia. This wasn't so bad.

"At least the soap and hot wax from the car wash didn't hit us," said Fiona.

Samantha agreed with Fiona's point.

Their sliding and flopping had thrown them into a new cement hallway, half as long and twice as wide as the entrance hall. Letters etched into the wall above the far end read:

STROOMDROGER

"Stroomdroger?" asked Lainey. "What could that possibly mean?"

Samantha stared at the word. Her uncle had taught her to say "Please," "Thank you," and "Where's the tallest building?" in eleven different languages. She had learned more words in many languages since she'd begun super-secret traveling, but this didn't mean anything to her.

"Power dryer," said Fiona. "It's Dutch."

"Dutch?" asked Lainey.

"Definitely," said Fiona. "I spent last summer on a detective camp train," she added as though that explained anything.

"What's a detective camp train?" asked Samantha.

"I think she means detective training camp," said Lainey.

"No," said Fiona. "It was a train. We rode around Europe and Asia, solving mysteries. We spent a day in the Netherlands."

Samantha was impressed. Traveling the world and looking for clues sounded like something she'd like to do some summer, too.

"Did anyone bring a little brother along?" Lainey asked.

Samantha took a moment to marvel at how incredibly specialized and focused Lainey was. This adventure definitely needed a little-brother expert, and she had found the right one.

"I don't know," Fiona answered. "I was looking out the window most of the time. Lead us to the *Stroomdroger*, Samantha."

Samantha, Fiona, and Lainey walked quickly down the hall, squishing as they went.

They passed through the opening labeled **STROOMDROGER** and into a new hallway where two clear chambers blocked their path.

The left chamber was a glass room, about the size of an elevator. On its front were sliding doors, and above the doors was a sign that said *VOOR MENSEN.*

The right chamber looked similar, but it was much smaller, about the size of a washing machine. A sign above its entrance said *VOOR KLEINE DIEREN.*

Samantha and Lainey looked at Fiona.

"For people," she said. "And for small animals."

"Impressive," said Samantha.

Lainey had already stepped forward to examine the larger chamber. She reached out a hand, and when her fingers passed in front of the doors, a red light flashed. A moment later a buzzer rang twice, and the sound of a huge turbine began to roar.

The last time she had heard a sound like that, Samantha was traveling in double-triple super-economy seats on an airplane, right by the engines.

The doors slid open, and Lainey shot Samantha and Fiona a surprised expression. She opened her mouth to speak, but before she could say anything, she was sucked into the big glass chamber.

Samantha stood motionless as she watched Lainey spin around the glass box like a paper cone in a cotton candy machine. She zipped past Samantha and Fiona, a startled look on her face, spun around the chamber three more times, and shot out at the other end of the hallway where a vent in the ceiling sucked her up like a vacuum, suspending her in the air for several seconds. Then it slowly and gently lowered her to the floor.

"Wow!" Lainey called through the two layers of glass. "Even my shoes are dry!"

She wore a huge smile on her face.

Fiona held out one arm.

"After you," she said to Samantha.

"Thanks," Samantha replied.

She stepped forward and waved a hand by the entrance. The red light flashed, and the huge turbine roared. Air gushed past her and then—

Ffff-wup!

A wave of suction yanked Samantha into the big glass chamber. She held on to her umbrella tightly as her hair whipped wildly and she twirled around inside the space. After three complete rotations, the doors slid open on the opposite side. Another blast of air forced her out into a new hallway. She floated briefly and then sank to the floor.

The trip through the *stroomdroger* wasn't as rough as she expected it to be, and Lainey was right: now she was completely dry.

Fans roared again, and Samantha felt a gust of air, then Fiona dropped gently beside her, dry and ready to go.

The hallway stretching ahead of them on this side of the *stroomdroger* chamber was much wider than the one on the other side.

"So amazing," said Lainey. "I never imagined there could be anything like this under Seattle."

"I suspect there are much stranger things ahead," Fiona told her.

She turned to look at Samantha.

"Am I right?" she asked.

Samantha shrugged. "Your guess is as good as mine," she answered.

She didn't want to give too much super-secret information away.

She checked to make sure her umbrella was secure over her shoulder. Uncle Paul had warned her that this part of Seattle wasn't on the Super-Secret Plans. It was comforting to have them with her, just the same.

CHAPTER TWENTY

UNSPECTACULAR SPECS

Samantha looked down. Close to her feet, a strand of mustard-colored yarn lay twisted on the floor. It looked just like the yarn she had seen outside by the Elephant Car Wash. The long strand continued along from the *stroomdroger* to a set of double doors at the far end of the room and continued, she assumed, out the other side.

"Nipper went that way," she said, pointing to the opening.

"That's probably the best choice," said Fiona. "Your brother likely didn't notice the secret door."

"What?" Samantha and Lainey both said at the same time.

Fiona pointed at the wall to her right.

"If you look carefully, there's a secret door," she said. "You can't see it right away because the hinges are built into the sides."

Samantha squinted at the wall. Two thin lines ran from ceiling to floor. She had missed the door completely, but Fiona had sized it up at a glance.

"Let's look for other clues," said Fiona.

Samantha saw that Lainey was still staring at the secret door.

"Little-brother clues," said Fiona.

Lainey turned around quickly.

Samantha smiled at Fiona. She seemed to have sized up Lainey, too.

Fiona took two steps, bent down, and ran her finger along the floor. She held it up for Samantha and Lainey.

"See? Flecks of silver paint," said Fiona. "You probably missed them because you were staring at that yarn. My guess is that a toy of some kind fell out of your brother's pocket here and rolled away."

Samantha squinted at Fiona's finger and could barely make out a few small silver particles. The real reason she missed it was probably because the tiny specks were practically invisible.

"Aren't you going to check the secret door?" Lainey asked. "Most little brothers can't stop themselves from touching and tapping and poking things. Especially secret doors."

"No," said Fiona. "I'm not getting a sense that Nipper is the kind of boy who pays enough attention to notice a door like that. Besides, there aren't any recent handprints, smudges, or marks on that secret door."

Samantha and Lainey both looked back at the wall. Fiona was right—the wall was free of smudges or marks.

"And of course, there is the trail of yarn," Fiona added. "Samantha, you made the right choice. Lead on."

As the three of them left the secret door behind and walked on down the hallway, Samantha marveled at how her sort-of, kind-of friend had so much self-confidence. On the other hand, *she* was the first person to spot the yarn trail.

The yellow yarn ran along the corridor as it turned to the left. The three walked around the corner. A few feet later, the yarn stopped just before the hallway came to an end at a new set of double doors. Samantha thought she could hear machines rumbling softly from the other side.

"Look," said Lainey, pointing to large metal letters pressed into the wall above the doors:

KOGELBAAN

Samantha and Lainey both turned to Fiona and waited.

"*Kogelbaan,*" Fiona said slowly. "I'm not certain, but it might mean 'marble track' . . . in Dutch. I've never encountered it before."

"Impressive," said Samantha.

"Multilingual," said Lainey.

"I'm a sesquipedalian, too," said Fiona.

"Sesqui-what?" asked Lainey. "Is that Dutch?"

"No," Fiona replied. "It's English. It means I use a lot of long words."

"Come on, guys," said Samantha, pushing open the double doors.

Immediately the soft motor sounds became a heavy mechanical rumble.

CHAPTER TWENTY-ONE

MYSTERY MACHINE

A room the size of Volunteer Park stretched out before the girls. Whirring and rumbling, a single gigantic machine filled the space. It reminded Samantha of a car factory she had seen in a video once. Contraptions moved back and forth, starting and stopping, turning and shifting in every direction. Instead of cars, though, gigantic marbles rolled along double-rail tracks.

Many of the tracks ran straight, while some curved, zigzagged, climbed, and dipped. On all sides, enormous marbles rolled out of view through circular exits, while new marbles entered the vast space through similar holes.

Each marble was a metal-and-glass sphere. Steel bands formed the frames, with curved glass windows between. They looked almost like industrial-strength hamster balls to Samantha—for six-foot-tall hamsters!

She looked closer at the balls as they passed. There was something yellow inside each one. They might be benches or padded sofas of some kind. The marbles moved too quickly for her to be sure.

"*Kogel-baan,*" said Fiona, as if checking off a list in her mind. "Dutch. Marble track."

Samantha smiled. She really had chosen the right people to help find her brother. Then she looked up and around the huge, clanking, moving room.

"How big do you think this whole thing is?" asked Lainey.

Samantha shrugged.

"I think this room is just one part of it," said Fiona. Her eyes darted around the space quickly. "There are twenty-six holes leading in or out of here," she added.

All three girls stood, transfixed by the massive marbles racing by.

"How come we've never heard anything about this before?" Lainey asked. "You'd think *somebody* would have said *something* about a giant marble coaster under Seattle."

Samantha still didn't have the foggiest idea how—or how much—to explain to Lainey and Fiona. Maybe that's part of the reason Uncle Paul didn't get very far. There are so many details! It's such a big story! Maybe it was time for her to start explaining everything—at least, a little bit of the little bit of everything that she knew. She glanced over her shoulder and took a deep breath.

"Okay," said Samantha, reaching for the umbrella.

A shadow passed overhead as a marble rolled on a track high above the girls. It continued in a straight line and came to a stop near an alcove at the end of the room. A cluster of lights glowed on a wall beneath the ball.

Samantha changed her mind. Fiona and Lainey didn't need to hear her whole story right now. She just needed them to help her find Nipper. She left the umbrella on her shoulder and pointed.

"Follow me," she said, and headed to the alcove.

They followed her as she crossed the room to a space about ten feet wide and ten feet deep. Set back into the wall, the massive machine wasn't quite as loud in here.

The three girls stopped and stared at a panel of lighted buttons. The numbers one through twelve glowed across four rows of three buttons each. A fifth row had only one button: the number thirteen.

"Uh-oh," said Lainey. "That's bad luck."

"Triskaidekaphobia," said Fiona, shaking her head.

"Triskai-what?" Lainey asked.

"That means fear of the number thirteen," Fiona explained. "You really should know that one for your little-brother research."

"You're right," said Lainey. "Two out of three little brothers are very superstitious."

"Nipper certainly is," Samantha added. "I remember when I tried to open my umbrella in the house, and he asked me not to do that because . . ."

She stopped herself. She had already decided not to say too much about her umbrella or her uncle or the RAIN or the SUN or the CLOUD. Or the WEATHER . . . whatever that was.

Samantha lowered her eyes. She spotted something close to the wall beneath the panel. At first, she thought she was looking at a pencil, but on closer inspection, it was another strand of yellow yarn.

She picked it up and handed it to Fiona.

"Can this tell us where Nipper went?" she asked. "It's the same color as the yarn we followed to get here."

"It might indicate something," said Fiona as she dropped the yarn to the floor. "But I bet there are other clues around, too."

Fiona knelt down and wiped her index finger along the floor, the way she had before.

"More paint. See?" she said, holding her finger out for the other girls.

Samantha squinted and nodded. "White," she said.

"So . . . ," said Fiona, standing back up. "I suspect your brother ran over to this panel . . . drawn to the glowing buttons. Does that sound right, Lainey?"

"Definitely," Lainey answered. "Little brothers are two to three times more likely to approach things that beep or blink or smell like—"

"Good," said Fiona, cutting her off.

She turned to face Samantha.

"How tall is Nipper?" she asked.

Samantha pictured her brother standing next to the magtrain mailbox, trying to peek inside the opening.

"About this high," she answered, holding her open hand level with her eyebrows.

"Okay," said Fiona. "Here's my theory."

She swung her arm across the button panel in an arc.

"I think he reached out, as I am doing now," Fiona continued, "and his finger passed over these three buttons. Ten, eleven, and twelve."

She repeated the gesture and stopped at the number thirteen.

"Of course, he probably didn't press *this* one," she said.

"Triskaidekaphobia," said Lainey.

Samantha nodded.

"So," Fiona continued, "Nipper reached for button thirteen and jerked his hand back. And that caused the white-painted object to fall out of his pocket."

Samantha nodded again. Fiona couldn't possibly know just how good Nipper was at losing things.

She saw that Fiona was busy scanning the floor.

"My guess is that your brother is dropping toy cars, and they keep rolling away," she said.

"Good guess," said Samantha.

"So . . . ," Fiona continued, "Nipper looked back up, and the numbers ten and twelve were at eye level for him. I give it a sixty-six percent chance he pushed button ten."

"Only sixty-six percent?" asked Samantha.

"Sixty-six point six, to be more exact," said Fiona.

Samantha was a little disappointed. After that long presentation, she'd hoped her master detective, sort-of, kind-of friend would be more certain.

"Of course," Fiona added, "that's based on what most people would do."

"Not in this case," said Lainey.

Samantha and Fiona looked at her.

"Little brothers aren't most people," Lainey continued. "And you missed something important."

Samantha smiled. This was all really interesting.

"Go on," said Fiona.

Lainey took a few steps to the right and pointed downward.

"That's an old piece of gum," she said, wiggling her foot above the spot. "Someone wearing tennis shoes stepped on it."

Fiona leaned over a little and eyed the spot from a distance.

"The marks are consistent with a boy's sneaker," she confirmed. "I can tell the gum has been there for a long time, two weeks or more."

Lainey knelt by the gum and took a plastic card from her pocket.

"Little brothers can't stop themselves from tapping or touching anything gross," said Lainey.

Samantha nodded in agreement.

Lainey used the card to pry the gum from the floor. She stood back up and waved the card with the gum in Samantha's face.

"Gross, right?" she asked.

"Exceptionally gross," Samantha replied.

"Continue, please," said Fiona.

Lainey pulled the gum off the card and handed the blob to Samantha, who took it reluctantly.

"Okay," said Lainey. "Your kid brother spotted the gum. He stepped on it, and then he bent down to poke at it. *That's* when the toy car fell out of his pocket."

"Wouldn't he try to find the toy?" asked Fiona.

"If he was paying attention, he would," Lainey answered.

"He wasn't," said Samantha. "And he didn't."

"Exactly," said Lainey. "And meanwhile, there's this big panel with glowing buttons."

She held out the card she had just used to lift the gum.

"Smell," she said.

Samantha and Fiona sniffed.

"Grape," said Fiona.

Lainey began sniffing the buttons, one by one. She stopped at button twelve and waved the girls over to investigate.

Samantha sniffed.

"Grape," she said.

"That's our button," said Lainey cheerfully.

"Okay. I'm impressed," said Fiona. "Have you ever been to any kind of detective camp?"

"No," Lainey answered. "But I've spent years studying little-brother behavior. Do you want to know the three most likely things a little brother says when he's in a car and a cow goes by?"

"There's a one hundred percent chance I don't," said Fiona.

Samantha smiled.

This was exactly why she asked both of them for help. She needed a master detective to piece together clues and a little-brother expert who really understood eight-year-old-boy brains.

Samantha realized she was still holding the blob of grape gum. She looked at it again. It made her think about Nipper. How far could he have gone? He must be pretty hungry by now. She decided not to toss it on the floor. She opened her purse, found a scrap of paper, and wrapped up the gum.

"Let's go," she said, dropping the gum into her purse and snapping it shut.

She pushed the button number twelve, and *clank!*

Everyone looked up as a magnet the size of a refrigerator dropped from a thick chain and latched on to the large marble above. There was a heavy grinding noise as the chain lowered the ball to rest on the floor in front of them. A circle-shaped section of the ball creaked as it swung open slowly.

Samantha looked in at the yellow object in the center of the ball. It *was* a sofa—a sofa on wheels. It rocked gently in the center of the ball.

"There's room for two in there," said Lainey, leaning forward. "Maybe three."

She stepped through the opening and sat down on the couch.

"Memory foam," she said.

Fiona hopped in next.

"Squishy," she said, pressing the bench with her palm.

Samantha followed, squeezed in between the two, and looked back at the open door. There was a silver handle in the center. She leaned out, grabbed it, and pulled the door shut.

Samantha sat back, and nothing happened.

She reached for the door handle again and twisted it.

Instantly the chain overhead rattled, and the ball jerked upward. They rode out over the center of the room.

Clank! The magnet let go and dropped them on a track. They landed with a jolt, but the sofa absorbed the shock.

"I like memory foam," said Fiona.

The three girls sat snugly packed into the couch as the ball started rolling along the track.

Samantha marveled at how the walls of the ball swirled around them while the sofa stayed upright.

"Wait a second," said Lainey.

She leaned over and reached past Fiona and Samantha. She grabbed the door handle and gave it a twist.

The ball skidded to a stop.

Lainey twisted the handle back, and the ball started rolling again.

"Okay. Got it," she said.

They rolled through the room, gaining speed quickly.

"I wonder," said Fiona. "How long is this ride?"

Samantha looked forward. They were headed toward one of the circular openings.

They rolled into a tunnel, and everything went dark.

CHAPTER TWENTY-TWO

BAAN VOYAGE

The darkness lasted for only a few seconds. Their ball rolled out of the tunnel and along a track that twisted and wound in all directions. Samantha figured that from high above the tracks, it must look like a bowl of spaghetti. Inside the ball, however, it felt like traveling through a giant pinball machine.

They banked left, right, and down an S-shaped section of track. When they hit a long steep straightaway, they gained speed, rolling faster and faster.

"Here comes a loop!" shouted Fiona, pointing straight ahead.

Samantha braced herself, expecting to flip upside down. Then she remembered how the outside of their ball moved around their foam bench. She and her friends faced forward as the ball zoomed up and around the loop-de-loop, resting comfortably on the sofa.

They reached another straight section of track, and Samantha had a chance to look around. They were just one of dozens of marbles on this part of the *kogelbaan*. Everywhere, empty steel and glass balls rolled over and around them on twisting rails. There didn't seem to be any way to know how many balls there were in all or just how big this bizarre coaster was. Were they still somewhere under Seattle?

"Here comes something new," said Lainey, pointing down at a huge circle.

"It looks like a pizza," said Fiona.

Their ball rolled off the end of the track and—*clank!*—dropped onto a huge round platform.

Samantha agreed that it really did look like a giant pizza, only instead of pepperoni, the surface was riddled with enormous ball-sized holes. The platform tilted left and right, and their ball wound around. They rolled over a hole and dropped again.

Clank!

They landed on a new track, rolled for a few seconds, and stopped.

"Is it over?" asked Fiona.

"I don't think so," said Samantha.

Clank! Clank!

More balls dropped from the pizzalike platter. Each one landed on a different section of track and then rolled out of sight behind them.

"We're just getting started," said Lainey, pointing over her shoulder.

Samantha glanced back and saw a huge stick aimed at their ball. It looked like a telephone pole lying on its side. Each ball that had rolled past them had lined up on a different track to push the stick farther back against a huge spring.

"It's loading up," Lainey added.

Samantha recognized this contraption. It was like a plunger from an impossibly huge pinball machine.

With a *crack!* the huge pole hit the back of their ball, and they shot forward. The spongy couch absorbed a lot of the shock—but not all of it. Samantha braced herself, gripping her umbrella tightly as they barreled into a new tunnel and the spaghetti chamber disappeared.

"This is the weirdest way in the world to travel," said Fiona.

Samantha wasn't sure about that. She had experienced many weird ways to travel recently. But rolling inside a giant marble machine was definitely a strange way to go . . . and she had no idea where they were going.

CHAPTER TWENTY-THREE

HAVING A BALL

"Holy cowabunga!" shouted Nipper. "This is an awesome way to travel!"

His ball zoomed through a triple loop, rolled up a steep hill, and picked up speed as it cruised down a long straight section of track. In the distance, the track curved upward and stopped. It formed a short ramp. Beyond, Nipper saw a vast field of enormous circles. They looked like giant bass drums.

"This is gonna be great," said Nipper, rocking his body to settle himself deeper into the squishy red bench.

He reached the ramp—and he was airborn!

Bing!

Bang!

Boing!

The ball bounced from drum to drum in giant arcs.

Clang!

He smacked down onto a new section of track and zoomed forward.

For a moment, Nipper thought he saw something standing on a ledge beyond the track. It might have been a person wearing a red helmet. But the marble was moving way too fast to get a good look.

As his ball rolled on and on, he wondered how long the ride would last. It had already been at least an hour. The ball banked around a long curved section of track and began to slow down.

To his right there was a wide flat surface. It reminded him of a subway station he'd seen in New York City. A staircase on the far end of the platform led to an opening with a sign on the wall next to it:

UITGANG:

ALLEN

PARK

Of the three words, Nipper recognized only one of them: *Park*.

"No way," he said. "I'm not parking."

This was too much fun. He checked the handle to make sure it was still turned all the way to the right. He didn't want the ball to stop rolling, ever.

Slowly he left the station behind.

He rolled down a short section of track, paused, and started moving forward again, climbing. It reminded Nipper of a roller coaster lift. He moved steadily up an impossibly big hill, so big that Nipper couldn't see the top of it. He glanced over his shoulder to see metal posts pushing his ball up the incline. It really was like the beginning part of a roller coaster ride . . . inside a big ball . . . underground!

The ball crested the top of the track and plummeted. The walls of the ball spun and spun as Nipper faced forward, eyes wide open. He had a double-triple super smile on this face. This was much better than traveling in yarn.

"Look out below!" he shouted.

Marble Coasters

Marble coasters, or rolling ball structures, are popular toys. People build the machines and race balls from start to finish using gravity, motors, and many clever mechanisms.

Made of wood, plastic, or metal, these toys have been around since the 1800s.

They are sold worldwide as construction sets for exploring physics, math, and creativity. In Dutch, a marble coaster is called a *kogelbaan*.

Many features of marble coaster design are seen in roller coasters and other amusement park rides today.

Of course, nobody—absolutely nobody—has ever said that riding a giant mechanical marble coaster would be an efficient, useful, convenient way to travel.

* * *

Look for symbols of a person inside a circle. These mark the entrances to the *kogelbaan*, a network of colossal marble coasters that roll beneath the continental United States.

Sealed inside a giant glass and steel sphere, you can zip, zigzag, and zoom from coast to coast.

The instructions for operating this system aren't very clear. And all the labels are in Dutch. However, in the *kogelbaan* you can reach many amazing places across the country.

Make sure to allow plenty of time for your return trip.

CHAPTER TWENTY-FOUR

THE NAME GAME

"When it comes to ball coasting, three things matter," said Crash Nitro. "Rotation, rotation, rotation!"

She waited. Thirteen members of the Clandestine League of Unstoppable Daredevils stood at attention. None of them laughed at her joke. She grunted softly. They never got any of her jokes.

"All right, then," she sighed. "Let's get down to business."

Crash Nitro pushed her helmet's face shield all the way up and shoved a tuft of colorful hair out of the way. The CLOUD watched her with visors open and eager smiles on their faces.

"Today, we're celebrating," said Crash Nitro. "Come on in . . . unstoppable daredevils."

The secret door opened, and two new recruits skipped into the room. Like everyone else, they wore bright blue jumpsuits and red helmets. They didn't yet have stickers on their helmets.

"You," Crash Nitro said to the one on her left. "Tell us all about your unstoppable stunt."

The recruit stepped forward.

"I scaled the Space Needle," she announced.

The CLOUD murmured with approval.

"And where is your proof?" asked Crash Nitro.

The daredevil held out a high-wattage lightbulb.

"I took one of the bulbs near the top of the tower," she said.

"A . . . lightbulb?" asked Crash Nitro, taking the item from her and trying not to sound disappointed.

She set it down and waved for the other recruit to step forward.

"You," said Crash Nitro. "What unstoppable stunt have you done?"

"I hooked a boogie board to the back of a ferry. Then I surfed across Puget Sound," he said proudly.

Again, happy whispers filled the hall.

"Unstoppable . . . ," said Crash Nitro. "Proof?"

The recruit held his arm straight out. A gold chain with a diamond dangled from his fist.

"I stole it from one of the passengers before I swam away," he told her.

Crash Nitro snatched the chain and carefully ex-amined the jewel hanging from it. It sparkled under the hall's fluorescent lights. It looked real. Good. She unzipped her fanny pack, dropped the bauble inside, and zipped it shut.

"Today, your unstoppable stunts have made you true daredevils," she said dramatically.

She reached into a pocket of her jumpsuit and took out two shiny white stickers shaped like clouds. She peeled the back off one sticker and slapped it on top of the first daredevil's helmet. Then she peeled the other sticker and slapped it onto the second recruit's helmet.

Even with all of their visors up, Crash Nitro couldn't properly see the CLOUD's faces, but she was sure they were giddy with enthusiasm.

"But wait," Crash Nitro said dramatically again. "There's more."

The room buzzed with excitement now.

"Bring out . . . the wheel!" she shouted.

Another daredevil pushed through the crowd, drag-ging a tremendous double prize wheel. Over eight feet tall, it featured a huge outer wheel and an inner wheel about half as big. Thirty-six sections displayed words on each wheel. Not just any words—double-triple super-action words.

Crash Nitro shoved both wheels as hard as she could.

"Jet fighter . . . hammerhead . . . hurricane," she called as the wheels spun.

She had done this dozens of times. It never failed to impress these silly men and women.

The double spinner whirred, clicked, and finally came to a stop.

"You!" she said, pointing to the recruit on her left. "You are now . . . Lightspeed . . . Firetruck!"

"Lightspeed Firetruck!" shouted the recruit, jumping up and down with excitement. "I'm Lightspeed Firetruck!"

Crash Nitro waited for her to settle down. Then she gave each wheel another big spin. It clicked loudly for a full minute before stopping.

"You!" she called as she pointed to the other recruit. "I name you . . . Bazooka . . . Mayhem!"

"Bazooka Mayhem!" cheered the brand-new CLOUD. "That's me!"

Crash Nitro waited for the crowd to settle down.

"All right," she said, rubbing her gloved hands together. "Let's get back to our crimes—I mean . . . our stunts."

The CLOUD waited. They all knew what was coming next.

Crash Nitro took a deep breath. Then she waved her arms even more dramatically than before.

"Bring out . . . the candy!" she shouted.

"Candy! Candy! Candy!" chanted the CLOUD.

Two daredevils wheeled a large steamer trunk in front of the group.

Crash Nitro kicked open the lid. Paper bags stuffed with candy filled the trunk in neat rows.

"Candy! Candy!" the CLOUD continued to chant.

"Eee-NUFF!" Crash Nitro shouted.

The CLOUD went silent instantly.

A daredevil in the front row raised his hand.

"Is there any gum in these bags?" he asked.

Crash Nitro reached into a pocket of her jumpsuit and pulled out a shiny metal boomerang, and the daredevil froze.

She raised the weapon and whipped it at him.

Swish!

The boomerang sailed past the daredevil's head.

Zip-zip-zip-zip . . .

It looped around the hall and returned to Crash Nitro.

. . . *smack!*

She caught it with one leather-gloved hand.

"I'm not giving away gum anymore!" she barked. "You clods keep dropping it on the floor!"

She lifted one foot and showed the bottom of her shoe to everyone. A dark gum circle clung to her sole.

"See?" she demanded.

Crash Nitro used the boomerang to scrape the gum from her boot. Then she lowered her foot and put the weapon back in her pocket.

"Any more questions?" she asked.

A daredevil in the second row raised her hand.

"I have a motorcycle," she said.

Crash shook her head.

"That's not a question," she sighed.

The daredevils kept watching her, but none of them moved.

Crash Nitro grunted. She had gone out of her way to recruit people who really followed directions. Unfortunately, this bunch was terrible at figuring out what to do *without* someone barking orders at them.

"Take your bags of candy, ride your marbles, and do your stunts across the USA!" she shouted.

One by one, the daredevils filed up to Crash Nitro, and she handed each a candy bag as they passed.

"Ride the track . . . bring something back!" they chanted as they marched through the secret door to the *kogelbaan*. "Ride the track . . . bring something back!"

Crash Nitro waited until the daredevils were all gone and she was alone, then she reached into another pocket of her jumpsuit.

She took out a worn photograph and studied it. Two kids—a boy and a girl—and a dog sprinted along a busy sidewalk in Capitol Hill. A mob of black-clad ninjas chased after them, waving swords.

Crash Nitro held the photo close to her face and squinted at the girl. She looked about eleven years old. In one hand, the girl clutched a bright red umbrella.

She snickered to herself, still staring at the girl in the photo.

"You've got plans . . . ," she said softly, ". . . and I've got plans."

Crash Nitro put the photo back in her pocket.

"To *take* your plans," she added.

CHAPTER TWENTY-FIVE

TURN LEFT, GO WRITE

From her seat on the yellow memory-foam sofa, wedged between Lainey and Fiona, Samantha watched the walls racing past their giant marble.

They banked left and right, over ramps, and under support beams. They corkscrewed and loop-de-looped. Over long stretches of double-rail track, they rolled slowly, slower than a person could walk. Then, suddenly, the track slanted down and they zoomed faster than a jet plane—or even a *slingshot trolley*. Samantha lost track of how far they traveled and had no idea where in the U.S. they could be.

"Under . . . where," Samantha murmured.

"I heard that," said Lainey.

Samantha looked sideways. She didn't realize that she'd spoken out loud.

"*Underwear* is one of the five most popular words among boys age six to ten," said Lainey.

"I don't see how that information is useful right now," said Fiona.

"Fine," said Lainey. "Do *you* have any useful information right now?"

Samantha could tell Fiona was doing some kind of calculation in her head.

"I'd guess we're five hundred miles from Seattle and two thousand five hundred miles behind Nipper," Fiona finished.

"Really?" asked Lainey.

"Yes," said Fiona. "Assuming Samantha's estimate—that her brother started five hours ahead of us—is accurate."

"So where do you think Nipper is now?" asked Samantha.

"I think he's on the East Coast," Fiona answered. "Based on our path so far, I'd say somewhere in New Jersey."

"That was genius," said Lainey.

"Thanks," said Fiona.

"You are *both* brilliant," said Samantha. "If anyone can help me find my little brother, it's definitely you two."

The ball lurched around another curve, shoving Samantha closer to Lainey.

"Now that we're talking about little brothers," said Lainey, "I have some more questions for you."

"Sure," said Samantha, smiling.

"How does your brother respond in dangerous situations?" she asked. "Does he make jokes about it? Does he look for food when he should be looking for safety? Can you think of a time when he had to accept help from a stranger?"

Samantha stopped smiling.

Had she mentioned that she and Nipper traveled a lot? Did she mention France? Did she mention Mali? She started thinking about Seydou.

"How about transportation?" Lainey continued. "Has anyone ever given you or Nipper a ride on a bicycle? Or a motorcycle?"

"Who? When?" Samantha sputtered. "Uh, no. I mean, no, I don't think so."

Samantha didn't say anything else. She looked straight ahead.

Their marble rose and fell, and they swerved around another sharp curve.

Trying not to draw any attention to herself, she opened her purse and took out Nipper's hand lens. She kept her hands low and hoped the other girls wouldn't notice. With her free hand, she pulled at one edge of the umbrella and tried to peek inside.

"Careful," said Lainey.

Samantha looked up quickly. She held her breath. Had Lainey seen anything?

"That was close," said Lainey. "For a second, I thought you were going to open that umbrella in here and bring us all bad luck."

Samantha exhaled. Lainey hadn't noticed. She really didn't want to make today any more complicated by having to explain everything—at least the part of everything she knew—to Lainey and Fiona.

She put the umbrella on her lap and opened her purse. She slid the hand lens back inside and took out her little black journal. She started to write:

Look for symbols of a person inside a circle. These mark the entrances to the . . .

"Taking notes?" Fiona said over her other shoulder.

Samantha held her breath again. Then she relaxed. There wasn't any reason to hide what she was doing.

"I'm writing about this ride," she told Fiona. "I want to record all the places we explore and add notes on how to get around."

Fiona nodded with approval.

"Good idea," she said. "It'll be interesting to see what you get when you put all your notes together."

Samantha remembered her uncle at the piano in New York.

"You can put lots of notes together and make a masterpiece," she said quietly so the other girls wouldn't hear her.

CHAPTER TWENTY-SIX

SHELL SHOCK

As Nipper's marble slowly rolled past a new station, he felt something rumble—his stomach. He picked another piece of yarn from his shirt. The mustard-yellow strand made him think of soft pretzels!

Peering through the ball's glass, he read a sign.

UITGANG:

MARGATE

CITY

Nipper had no idea where he was, but he was more than ready for a break. He had been coasting for at least five hours, and the last thing he had to eat was birdseed.

"I'll grab a snack . . . and come right back," said Nipper, reaching for the handle.

He twisted it, and the ball skidded to a stop. He pushed the door open and climbed onto the platform. Then he headed up a flight of steep narrow stairs. At the top, he opened a door and saw . . . an elephant.

"Wait. What? Waitaminute," Nipper said.

A three-story building towered over him—and it was shaped like an elephant! The big gray structure had a red middle section dotted with windows that made the elephant look like it was wearing a blanket. He had come out of a door in one of the elephant's legs. A few yards away, an iron fence surrounded the building, supporting a sign over the gate:

WELCOME TO LUCY

"Nifty," said Nipper. "Waitaminute," he said again, looking around.

All four legs of the elephant building had doors. He didn't want to forget which one led to the ball station, so he took out the stack of stickers Uncle Paul had given him. They had pictures of funny food packages on them. He looked around for a good spot to stick one to the door so he could find the ball coaster again.

Nipper smiled. He was thinking like Samantha now.

Crack! "Yow!" he cried, rubbing his cheek.

Something had hit Nipper in the face.

He looked around. He'd dropped all his stickers. As he bent down to pick them up, he spotted something small and orange . . . and peanut shaped.

"A candy circus peanut," he said.

The last time Nipper had seen one of those sad candies, it had been fired at him by a clown . . . in a theater . . . in New York City.

"Where did that come from?" he said, looking left and right.

Crack!

Another orange projectile sailed past his head and bounced off the elephant's belly. Nipper looked across the lot and under the structure.

A monkey sprang from behind one of the front legs.

It was the ninja monkey from the RAIN!

Who was also the "Great Flingo" from Buffy's Broadway play!

The animal clutched a strange silver machine with both hands. Nipper recognized the device immediately. It was a circus-peanut gun from the SUN. Somehow, that monkey had escaped—and gotten away with a peanut launcher, too!

"*Breep!*" the monkey screeched.

Crack! Crack!

Two more peanuts flew past Nipper and bounced off the door behind him. He spotted a new door on one of the elephant's other legs and dashed toward it.

Crack! Crack! Crack!

Nipper pulled the door open. A spiral staircase twisted up through the elephant's leg. He dashed inside and sped around and up and around and up. He heard footsteps behind him as he reached the top and opened a door.

Crack! Crack! Crack!

A hailstorm of candy peanuts followed him through the doorway. He dove out of the way.

Crack! Crack!

Peanuts cascaded across the floor in every direction.

Crack! Crack!

More peanuts flew past his face, and candy ricocheted around the room.

"Breep!"

Nipper looked back and saw the monkey standing in the doorway. He pushed himself up, ran back to the entrance, and slammed the door.

The room was silent.

"How . . . incredibly . . . awful!" he panted.

Nipper bent forward, rested his hands on his thighs, and slowly caught his breath. Then he looked around the room.

Wood paneling lined the walls, and sunlight streamed in from a window in the center of the high vaulted ceiling. Posters with black-and-white photos stood on tripods.

On one wall, a big canvas stretched across a metal frame. It showed an illustration of Lucy the Elephant. Nipper guessed it had been drawn when the building was new, because of the old-fashioned cars in the scene. On the opposite wall, a framed map had the words *Atlantic City, New Jersey* carved into fancy wooden frame. If he hadn't known it already, Nipper would never have guessed that he was inside an elephant building. It looked like a room in any old museum.

He took a deep breath and relaxed.

Nipper walked to the back of the room and looked out a window. There was a street nearby, and a few parked cars. He heard ocean waves.

"I'm peeking out of an elephant's butt," he chuckled, and headed back to the front of the room.

He walked to the elephant's head and hopped several times, trying to look through a round window high up on the wall. He wanted to peek out of the elephant's eye, but he was too short. He looked back around the room. Circus peanuts lay everywhere. He began gathering the candy.

Knock-knock!

Nipper froze. He eyed the door nervously. He held his breath and tried not to make a sound.

Knock-knock!

Nipper couldn't stop himself.

"Who's there?" he called.

"Breep."

"Breep who?" Nipper asked.

"Breep!"

The monkey kicked open the door with one of its hairy feet. The peanut gun was gone. Instead, the primate waved a samurai sword wildly with one hand.

Swi-thunk!

The monkey threw a *shuriken*—a ninja throwing star— with the other hand. It sailed past Nipper and stuck into wood-paneled wall behind him.

Nipper reached for the picture of Lucy the Elephant, yanked it off the wall, and charged at the monkey.

Ka-scrunch!

Nipper swung the frame down onto the horrible ninja beast. The monkey's head ripped through the canvas, but the metal frame pinned its hairy arms to its body.

To Nipper, it looked like a portrait of an elephant with the head of a monkey. It would have been hilarious . . . if it weren't so incredibly awful!

"Breep!" the monkey howled again.

It struggled to swing its samurai sword but couldn't free its arms.

Nipper shoved the framed animal sideways, then raced down the stairs and out of the building. He looked left and right. Where were his stickers? He couldn't remember which of the elephant legs led to the marble coaster.

Suddenly a tiny circle with a person in the center caught his eye.

He sprinted to that door, opened it, and charged into the *kogelbaan* station.

CHAPTER TWENTY-SEVEN

IT WASN'T FAIR

"Truck fourteen! Truck fourteen!"

Buffy watched her mother struggling with the wheel of the giant eighteen-wheel flatbed.

"Truck fourteen! Truck fourteen!"

"Oh, Mother," said Buffy, ignoring the blaring radio. "I feel like Nelly McPepper." She raised a hand to her forehead dramatically. "My life has become drab and tragic," she whined.

"Truck fourteen! Do you copy?"

"Someday, a bestselling author is going to write a book about my life," she continued. "I know exactly what I'm going to call this chapter."

"Let me guess," said her mother, working the truck

controls. "How about . . . 'I Was in Big, Big Trouble for Skipping School'?"

The radio crackled and blared again:

"Truck fourteen! The Dazzling Dozen is at the rendez-vous point near Atlantic City! Trucks will be loading soon and ready to go!"

"Dazzling Dozen?" Dr. Spinner asked Buffy.

"Yes, Mother," she answered. "Those trucks hold thousands of exquisite shoes and accessories . . . enough to fill a museum. I simply had to give them a fabulous Broadway-star name."

"Broadway?" asked Dr. Spinner. "Trucks don't star on Broadway."

"Of course they do," said Buffy. "Didn't you see *Scarlett Hydrangea's Secret of the—* Oh. I forgot. *You* were busy saving Samantha from clowns and a giant lizard. You missed the whole thing."

"Your father and I were kidnapped, and we were tied up with yarn," said Dr. Spinner.

"That's a bizarre and improbable tale," said Buffy.

Her mother didn't answer. She concentrated on steering the truck as they turned off the Atlantic City Expressway.

Buffy looked at herself in the rearview mirror. She started to adjust her hair when something caught her eye. For a split second, she thought she saw a boy . . . running around an elephant . . . chased by a monkey.

"How awful," she said. "Mustard yellow is a hideous color to wear any season of the year."

They reached the warehouse complex where the Dazzling Dozen waited in a long rumbling line. Minutes later, they were in the lead truck of a mighty truck convoy, rolling out of Margate City.

"Buffy, I've been wondering about something," said Dr. Spinner. "Why are we truck fourteen when there are only thirteen vehicles?"

"Muh-thurrrrr," said Buffy. "Everyone knows that thirteen is an unlucky number. We can't drive all the way back to the West Coast in a bad-luck truck!"

CHAPTER TWENTY-EIGHT

DON'T PUG ME

"Okay. You can open your eyes now, George."

George Spinner opened his eyes. A long staircase had appeared where the mailbox used to be. He followed his brother's voice and headed down the cement steps. At the bottom, Paul waited for him in a dimly lit room.

"Where's Dennis?" George asked.

"He's still outside," Paul answered. "You know he doesn't enjoy your shoes."

His brother looked past his shoulder toward the staircase.

"Come on, Dennis," he called. "Let's take the train and see what we're missing!"

The sound of plastic clattering against cement echoed around the room as Dennis trotted down the stairs.

George tried to make out details of the chamber he'd entered. The walls curved around him, and there were several exits, but it was definitely too dim to see much more.

"Stay close," said Paul, pointing at the entrance to a tunnel. "Very little light reaches down from the street."

"Not a problem," said George. "Show 'em what you can do, old pal."

"Wruf!" Dennis barked.

Instantly a powerful bolt of light blazed from the pug's cone.

"Gah!" yelled Paul, shielding his eyes.

"I replaced the ordinary lightbulb with my X-27B," said George. "As you can see, it's very high candlepower."

Dennis swung his head back and forth. The light, amplified by the cone, was remarkably bright. Steam rose from the wall wherever the beam lingered.

"The combination of light and cone seems to have created a super-beacon dog," said George.

"Is this really necessary?" asked Paul, shielding his eyes as he reached down and felt around for the Blinky Barker.

"What are you doing?" asked George.

"I'm looking for a button," said Paul. "Doesn't this thing have a button?"

He closed his eyes and began to fumble around the collar with both hands.

"Why would you invent something like this without a *button*?" Paul complained.

"I already told you," said George. "I didn't invent the Blinky Barker. I bought it at the pet expo a few months ago."

Bzzt! Zzzzzzzzzzzt!

George's shoes went off. Dennis scampered away.

"Watch," said George, glancing down at his heels.

"Watch what?" asked Paul.

"No," he answered. "My dog clogs just reported that Nipper dropped a watch."

In the distance, Dennis's super beacon flashed. The pug was already far ahead of them in the tunnel.

CHAPTER TWENTY-NINE

SHOW AND SMELL

Dennis trotted along the hallway.
Everything was very bright.
It was hard to see.

He heard the men following him.
He would lead them to the train.
He liked train rides.

Dennis liked the man in the orange shoes.
He dropped waffles.
Dennis liked the man in the beeping shoes.
He also dropped waffles.

But Dennis did not like the beeping shoes.
They hurt his ears.

Dennis walked ahead of the men.
He walked as far ahead of the beeping shoes as he could.
He really wanted to get away from the beeping shoes.

CHAPTER THIRTY

INSIDE, OUTSIDE, UPSIDE DOWN

Nipper darted down the stairs to the Margate City *kogelbaan* station. In the distance, he saw a ball coasting toward the platform. It rolled up and down a hill-shaped section of track, losing speed, and rolled slowly up to the platform.

Nipper reached out and grabbed the door handle. He gave it a twist, and the ball stopped. He pulled open the door.

Swi-clack!

A silver blade narrowly missed his shoulder. Sparks flew as it connected with the metal frame of the ball.

Nipper turned around.

"Breep!"

The horrible monkey howled at him, inches from his face. He smelled marshmallows on the animal's breath—but it didn't make him hungry at all! The monkey flailed both of its hairy arms in the air. In one hand he waved the samurai sword. In the other hand he clutched a dozen of the funny stickers Nipper had dropped outside the elephant building.

Nipper jumped backward into the ball.

The monkey jumped into the ball after him.

Nipper jumped forward out of the ball, turned, and slammed the door shut, trapping the monkey inside.

"*Breep!*" screeched the monkey, banging on the round glass door with his sword.

Nipper gave the handle a twist, locking the door.

"So long, sucker!" he shouted.

The ball didn't move.

Inside, the screaming monkey was standing on the bench, holding on to the frame, stopping the ball from turning.

Nipper watched the monkey for a moment. Then he stepped onto the track behind the ball with one foot on each rail. With both hands, he gripped one of the ball's metal bands and pushed upward with all his might. The ball started to turn.

At the same time, the monkey let go of the frame on the inside. The ball lurched forward, and Nipper didn't have time to let go. Still holding on to the frame, the movement carried him up to the top of the ball as it turned. Now he really couldn't let go!

"*Yaaaaaaaaaaaaah!*" Nipper screamed, rolling over and down.

He passed between the rails and rode up again—and down again. And up. And down again.

The ball left the station with a boy riding *outside* the frame. The angry ninja monkey inside punched at the yellow leather sofa with its hairy fists.

CHAPTER THIRTY-ONE

NEWS OF THE WHIRLED

"Did I ever tell you about the time I climbed up the *outside* of the Statue of Liberty?" asked Supersonic Starship.

"Yes," said Lightning Hot Potato. "Fifty times. But did I ever tell *you* about the time I skateboarded through the Library of Congress . . . on one leg . . . with my eyes closed?"

"Only two hundred times . . . in the past week alone," Supersonic Starship replied.

The two CLOUD daredevils sat beside one another at the edge of the *kogelbaan* platform, taking a break, eating candy and watching the balls go by.

Lightning Hot Potato popped a malted milk ball into her mouth. She chewed it and swallowed.

"What are we looking for, again?" she asked.

"An umbrella," said Supersonic Starship. "The boss says we should keep an eye out for a girl with a red umbrella."

Lightning Hot Potato nodded while she ate a handful of tangerine jelly beans.

"Why?" she asked when she was done chewing.

"I'm not really sure," said Supersonic Starship. "For the past few weeks, all she talks about is that umbrella, and how much she wants us to . . . Hey! Don't eat all the best candy on the first day. Save some for the rest of the trip."

Lightning Hot Potato swallowed.

"How long is this trip going to last?" she asked.

"Thirteen days," Supersonic Starship answered.

He watched Lightning Hot Potato pick a gummy bear from her bag and eat it.

"I'm warning you," he told her. "Keep it up, and you're not going to have anything left except *sad candy*."

"*Breep!*"

Both daredevils looked up. A ball rolled past them. Inside, a monkey screamed and banged a samurai sword against the glass.

"*Yaaaaaaaaaaaaah!*"

Outside, a boy rode *on* the ball.

"Whoa, Nelly!" shouted Supersonic Starship.

"I can't believe it!" shouted Lightning Hot Potato.

"We've got to follow him!"

"We've got to tell everyone about this!"

The two daredevils jumped into the next marble.

"Tell them all . . . there's a boy on a ball! Tell them all . . . there's a boy on a ball!" they both chanted as they cruised down the track.

CHAPTER THIRTY-TWO

POUR NIPPER

"*Yaaaaaaaaaah!*"

Over and over Nipper went, clinging to the ball with all his strength.

To his right, he saw a new platform. Then he went under the ball.

He saw the platform again. Then he went under the ball.

He saw the platform again—and he jumped.

He landed and fell to his knees, panting.

"*Breep!*" the monkey screeched.

Nipper turned and watched the ball roll away. The monkey was still inside, banging on the glass with its sword. He kept watching until the ball disappeared from sight completely. Then he collapsed on the platform, facedown.

Suddenly he sat up. He looked down the track again to make sure the horrible ninja monkey had really gone. The track was clear. He let out a sigh of relief and lay back down on the floor to rest. Every few minutes, he heard the soft rumble of a new ball rolling past the station.

Something rumbled even louder.

It was his stomach.

Across the platform, a sign hung on the wall next to a staircase.

UITGANG:
BEDFORD

"Why is every place I go called *Uitgang?*" he wondered out loud as he headed to the exit.

He trudged up the stairs, pushed open a door . . . and saw an elephant-sized coffee pot!

A two-story building rose in the distance. It was round and silver with a large spout near the top. The structure had a big red handle and a few windows set in red frames.

Nipper knew the building was supposed to be a coffee pot. It had the words THE COFFEE POT painted on it in big letters. A door underneath the big silver spout stood open. He didn't really like coffee, but maybe there were snacks inside, too.

As he crossed the street, he picked at another strand of yellow yarn. It made him think of lemon bars.

Bop!

Something hit Nipper in the face.

He looked down. A candy circus peanut lay on the ground at his feet. He looked up. Two people in jumpsuits and motorcycle helmets waved at him enthusiastically.

"Hey!" shouted one of them. "We want to talk to you!"

They started walking toward Nipper. He turned and ran.

"Come back!" one of them called. "We've got candy!"

Nipper already had seen what kind of candy they were throwing. Sad candy. No thanks. This had to be some kind of trick.

"You're a superstar!" he heard the other one shout.

Nipper kept running. A ninja throwing star had almost killed him already today. He didn't want to find out about any more stars!

He ignored his rumbling stomach as he dashed back across the street, through the doorway, and down the stairs to the ball coaster.

CHAPTER THIRTY-THREE

COFFEE BREAK

"*Buffy, I am now telling you something that is important not to forget. It was a terrible idea to leave California without telling your high school. You need to start living life in a way that you don't make so many bad decisions. Learning can actually be fun. Trust me, getting a good education can be as exciting as a Broadway play or a movie.*"

Suzette Spinner, DVM, took a deep breath and let out a heavy sigh. This was the third time she'd recited that speech to Buffy. She was pretty sure her daughter was listening to only every thirteenth word.

She had become comfortable behind the wheel of the massive flatbed truck. It was easier than she thought to lead a convoy of eighteen-wheelers across the U.S. Getting a teenager to listen to you, however, was much, much harder.

"Maybe I should donate all my shoes and accessories to a museum," Buffy sighed as she stared out the window.

Pango-lango-lango-langolin! Pango-lango-lango-langolin!

From inside the glove compartment, Dr. Spinner's phone rang loudly.

"Hold on," she said, leaning forward.

She worked the truck's turn signals, glanced at both side mirrors, then put her weight into the steering wheel. The truck lurched onto the exit ramp.

"Mother!" said Buffy, pointing back to the highway. "The Dazzling Dozen is getting away!"

"We'll catch up with them, dear," said Dr. Spinner, activating the air brakes. The big rig hissed as it slowed to a halt. "Please hand me my phone."

Buffy turned the knob, and the glove compartment panel flopped open. She grabbed the phone and tossed it to her mother.

"Thank you," said Dr. Spinner.

"You still don't understand anything important," said Buffy, turning back to the window.

"Hi, dear," Dr. Spinner told the phone. "Yes. This is Suzette. Who did you think it would be?"

She sighed gently and rolled her eyes, but her daughter was looking the other way.

"Did you have something you wanted to tell me, George?" she asked.

Her husband rambled on about socks and dogs. He eventually asked about her current location.

"We've stopped in a city called Bedford," she said. "Oh? You've heard of it? There's a giant coffee pot nearby?"

"Look, Mother," Buffy interrupted. "I see a boy crossing the street. I think it's Nipper."

"Hold on," Dr. Spinner told her husband.

She looked over her daughter's shoulder. She saw two people in helmets and jumpsuits, but no Nipper.

"George," she said into the phone. "Buffy thinks she just saw Nipper out here. That's not possible, is it?"

Her husband started talking about electronics and math. It sounded like he was agreeing with her.

"Never mind, Mother," said Buffy. "There are so many badly dressed people, it's hard to tell them apart."

"Was there something important you wanted to tell me, George?" asked Dr. Spinner.

Her husband had already hung up.

Dr. Spinner sighed again and gave the phone back to Buffy. She put the truck in gear, steering the massive flatbed rig off the shoulder and onto the on-ramp.

"Make sure none of my accessories get jostled," said Buffy.

"Yes, dear," said Dr. Spinner.

"And we should stop every five hundred miles to pol-
ish all the silver," said Buffy. "Tarnish is tragic."

Dr. Suzette Spinner gritted her teeth and gripped
the steering wheel with both hands. She took a deep
breath and started her speech once more.

"Buffy, I am now telling you something that is important not to forget. It was a terrible idea to leave California
without telling your high school. . . ."

The Coffee Pot

A giant coffee pot welcomes visitors to Bedford, Pennsylvania.

This two-story, pot-shaped building is a celebrated example of novelty architecture. It was originally built in 1927 as a roadside café, serving ice cream, sandwiches, and, of course, coffee to customers of a gas station. It has been remodeled since then, and moved to a clearing on the Bedford County fairgrounds, where it remains a happy sight for passersby.

If it were a real coffee pot, it could hold 819,000 cups of coffee!

The Ketchup-Bottle Water Tower

A water tower in the shape of a giant ketchup (also called "catsup") bottle rises over the highway near Collinsville, Illinois.

The "bottle" is seventy feet tall, perched on one-hundred-foot steel legs. If it really were a ketchup bottle, it could hold one hundred thousand gallons of sauce!

Built in 1949 to advertise the Brooks Catsup Company, the giant tower has become a favorite sight for visitors to Collinsville, and many others on their way west to St. Louis, Missouri.

* * *

Both of these landmarks are near stations for track 12 of the *kogelbaan*. You can roll from Bedford to Collinsville in about an hour.

It's really important to study the *kogelbaan* map, however. If you don't get off at Collinsville, the next station is Cawker City, Kansas. These two cities are only about five hundred miles apart by car. But if you're making the trip using track 12 of the *kogelbaan*, the twisting, turning trail between these two stops is more than twenty-two thousand miles long! You'll be inside a ball for over a week!

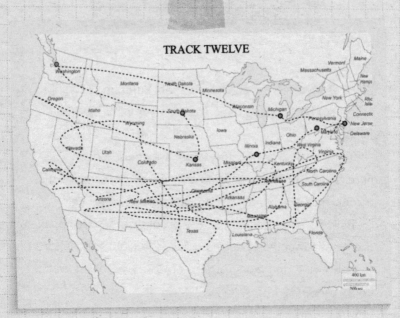

TRACK TWELVE

Many super-secret travel networks can be used for speedy travel around the world, but this is definitely not one of them. If you don't get off the *kogelbaan* at the right stop, you could be in for a very long ride.

Unlike the magtrain, or the slidewalk, it's clear that the people who designed and built the *kogelbaan* didn't really spend a lot of time communicating and coordinating with each other. They didn't cooperate or work well together at all.

So if you're in a hurry to travel across the U.S., you're much better off driving, biking, taking a bus, or even using some form of novelty motorized, wheeled transportation to get where you want to go.

CHAPTER THIRTY-FOUR

TRACK OR TREAT

The marble slowed as it rolled past a long platform. Samantha could see a doorway at the far end of the platform with stairs leading up and out of sight.

It reminded her of the subway stations in New York City.

"Let's stop here and look around," she said.

She reached for the handle in their marble's round door and gave it a quick twist. The ball came to a stop, and she pushed the door outward.

"*Uitgang* means exit," said Fiona, pointing at the sign on the wall.

UITGANG:

ALLEN

PARK

"Allen Park, Michigan," said Lainey. "That's where you can find the world's biggest tire."

"Why would you even know that?" asked Fiona.

"If you want to be an expert on brothers, you have to learn a whole lot of useless facts," Lainey answered.

Samantha thought about telling Lainey to join WRUF, the Worldwide Reciters of Useless Facts. She changed her mind.

"Do you think there's any chance Nipper got off the ride here?" asked Samantha.

"Possibly," said Fiona. "Your brother sounds like one of those boys who get hungry a lot."

"No," said Lainey. "He kept rolling."

"How do *you* know that?" Fiona asked.

Lainey opened her hand, revealing a dozen miniature gears, screws, and other tiny items.

"I've been collecting little bits of machinery from the ground," she explained. "I found some of it along the way to the *kogelbaan*. I don't see anything similar here. So I don't think Samantha's brother got out of his ball at this station."

Samantha and Fiona looked at the shiny items in Lainey's palm.

"Okay," said Fiona. "But how do you even know they're from Sam's brother?"

Lainey turned to Samantha.

"Did your brother ever carry a pocket watch?" she asked.

"Maybe," she answered. "Are you thinking it's a really fancy pocket watch?"

"Very likely," Lainey answered. "Most of these pieces seem to be gold, and there are some tiny jewels, too. They might be sapphires."

Samantha could see that some of the tiny bits sparkled.

"And . . . does it look like somebody let it drop and break into thousands of pieces?" Samantha asked.

"It seems that way," said Lainey.

"Then yes," said Samantha. "My brother carried that pocket watch."

"All right, then," said Lainey, heading back to the track. "Let's go look for boys!"

Samantha and Fiona didn't move.

"I mean look for *a* boy," Lainey said, "singular."

Samantha shook her head, but she smiled a little, too. It was kind of funny.

"Wait," said Fiona, suddenly sounding worried. "Come here."

She stood by the exit sign, pointing to something. Samantha and Fiona walked over and joined her.

They saw a map of the U.S. painted on the wall to one side of the exit. One long, meandering dotted line

172

connected seven circles. The number twelve appeared in each corner of the map.

"These are the seven stations of track twelve," said Fiona. "We're in Michigan, right here."

Samantha spotted the state of Michigan easily. Anyone could. It looks like a mitten.

"There are six more stops before we get back to Seattle," Fiona noted.

"Got it," said Lainey. "What's the problem?"

Fiona began to trace the line with her finger.

"So far, we've been traveling *mostly* in a straight line," she explained. "There have been a lot of curves and loops, but it's been a direct path, more or less."

She moved her finger along the line until she got to the fourth circle.

"That all ends here," said Fiona. "St. Louis."

Samantha watched Fiona's finger as she traced the dotted line. The path twisted and turned, winding back and forth across the U.S. before it finally reached another circle.

"There are three more stops in the next few hours," Fiona calculated. "After that, there's a whole week before there's another chance to get out of a ball."

"A week?" asked Samantha.

That was a long time for super-secret travel. The magtrain and slidewalk never took longer than an hour or two at the most. Samantha made a mental note to ask her uncle about this, too, when she got home . . . and had a chance to learn about *everything*.

"I promised my parents I'd be home by dinner," said Lainey. "I'm in trouble."

"I know, I know," said Fiona. "With my schedule, I can't stay away from Seattle for a week, either."

"Sam?" asked Lainey. "What about your little brother?"

"If he stopped at a station, do you think he paid attention and noticed the map?" asked Fiona.

"Unlikely," Samantha and Lainey both said at the same time.

"Do you think he can stay in the ball for days and days without getting bored?" asked Lainey.

"He can't," said Samantha and Lainey at the same time.

Samantha tried to picture her brother in one of those locations by himself. He *might* be able to get home. Or . . . he might annoy someone and get chopped into cubes. Or attacked by a clown or a dangerous animal or a pirate. Or he might get flushed into a bottomless pit.

"Okay, Lainey," said Samantha. "Based on everything you know, what's the absolute farthest station a boy would ride to before he got bored, started fidgeting, and got out?"

Lainey joined her in front of the map. She traced the dotted line with her finger.

"Fun . . . fun . . . ," she said as she traced. "Fun . . . not-so-fun . . . boring."

Her finger stopped at a circle between Illinois and Missouri.

"Too bad there's no shortcut between these stations," Fiona mused out loud. "Whoever built this system really didn't think about—"

"Wait," Samantha interrupted. "Why is that too bad?"

Fiona pointed to their location on the map again.

"If we could just skip from here to Mitchell or Cawker City, then we could roll home in a few hours instead of seven days," she said.

"Seven Days!" wailed Lainey.

While Fiona and Lainey stared at the map, Samantha walked to the edge of the platform. She wanted to be as far away from the other girls as she could without drawing attention to herself.

"I'm going to be in so much trouble," she heard Lainey moan.

"I think we'll start dying of thirst . . . about . . . here," she heard Fiona explain in a matter-of-fact voice.

Samantha opened her umbrella and put it on the floor. She pulled out Nipper's hand lens. This was an emergency. She had to work quickly. She studied the lining until she found what she needed and quickly snapped the umbrella shut.

"Okay, girls," she called. "I know a shortcut."

She pointed at them with her umbrella.

"But it's super-secret."

CHAPTER THIRTY-FIVE

WHEELIE? SINCE WHEN?

"The Uniroyal Giant Tire," said Lainey.

Samantha and her friends stood in a field beside a highway near Allen Park, Michigan. The world's biggest tire loomed above them. It looked exactly like a car tire—if the car it belonged to was the size of the RMS *Titanic*.

Samantha stared at the massive treads that zig-zagged up the sides of the huge wheel. She squinted at the giant letters along the top spelling UNIROYAL, each one as tall as a person. She gazed at the enormous sunburst-shaped hubcap. The sunburst alone was probably forty feet across. Then she looked over at the immense shadow the giant landmark cast across the field.

Unfortunately, she had no idea how this colossal tire offered a super-secret shortcut.

"If you write about this in your notes, Samantha," Fiona observed, "you'll probably have to use eight different synonyms for the word *giant*. Maybe more."

When she had looked at the Plans, Samantha had spotted the number fifteen in a circle . . . inside the state of Michigan. Lines pointed from the circle to several other U.S. states. What could it possibly mean?

Samantha was sure that if Nipper were here, he'd make an annoying suggestion that wasn't helpful at all, and then she'd argue with him, and she'd wind up figuring out what to do by accident. It almost always seemed to work out that way.

"So," said Lainey. "Are we going to ride in a big wheel?"

In the past few months, Samantha had become very good at deciphering her umbrella's secret instructions. This one was a puzzler for sure, but she knew she could do it. She kept staring up at the giant tire.

Fiona tapped her on the shoulder.

"Can we climb into that pit now?" she asked. "I see some interesting vehicles in the center."

"Huh?" Samantha asked, turning to look.

Fiona was pointing to the field. The dark shape next to the tire only *appeared* to be its shadow. It was actually a round pit, about the same diameter as the tire itself. It looked as deep as the tire was wide. And in the middle of the circle, parked on the gravel floor, four strange machines were parked in a line.

"Tricky," said Samantha, looking from the giant tire to the giant hole. "I was looking right at it and I didn't notice."

"That's the kind of thing most little brothers wouldn't ever notice," added Lainey.

"True," said Fiona. "But I think *most* people don't take a closer look at things like this."

Samantha didn't say anything, but she couldn't agree more.

The three girls walked to the edge of the pit. A ladder led down into it.

Fiona gestured for Samantha to go first. Then she waved to Lainey. One after the other, they began the climb down into the pit.

"If I had a little brother with me right now," Lainey said as she descended, "he probably would have raced ahead or run off looking for snacks and vanished."

As Samantha stepped from rung to rung she marveled about how much Lainey seemed to know about brothers. What else was she going to figure out?

Finally, at the bottom of the ladder, she hopped off and landed on the gravel surface with a *crunch*, followed by two more *crunch*es as Fiona and Lainey landed beside her.

From down in the pit Samantha could get a better look at the four strange machines resting on a paved square in the center of the circle.

"Lainey was correct before," said Fiona.

"Correct about what?" Samantha asked quickly.

Had both of her friends started figuring out her secrets . . . about her travels and ninjas and clowns . . . and Seydou?

"Lainey was correct that we *are* going to ride in big wheels," said Fiona.

She pointed out of the pit to the giant tire.

"Just not that one," she added.

Samantha looked more closely at the four vehicles standing in front of them. Each was basically a single big tire. It was narrow and about seven feet tall, with a seat in the center connected to a steering wheel like a car.

"I know what these are," said Lainey. "They're monocycles."

"Is that from your little-brother research?" asked Fiona.

Lainey walked up to one of the vehicles and pointed to the top of wheel. She pointed down to the bottom of the wheel. In both places was the word MONO-CYCLE.

"You got me," said Fiona. "I was the one who didn't take a closer look at things that time."

Samantha followed Lainey to the big wheels and hopped into a seat in the closest vehicle. In the center of the steering wheel was a white sunburst. It matched the hubcap of the giant tire above them. She looked down and saw that a small kickstand kept the monocycle upright. She rested her feet on pedals that stuck out below the seat and pressed the sunburst. It began to blink, and the engine started.

She expected a loud roar, like a motorcycle or a race car. Instead, the monocycle hummed like an electric toothbrush.

"Electric," said Fiona, hopping into the vehicle next to her.

Samantha waited until she saw Lainey sit down inside another monocycle. Then she used her right foot to pull up the kickstand and press down on the foot pedal. The big wheel took off.

She began to drive around the circular pit. There didn't seem to be any way out other than the ladder. She kept driving, searching for any sign of an exit.

When she completed a lap around the pit, Lainey and Fiona joined her. Side by side, the three girls drove their monocycles around the circle.

"Any idea how we're supposed to leave?" Lainey called.

Fiona shook her head, and Samantha looked up past Fiona's monocycle, out of the pit toward the giant tire. She noticed again how the sunburst on her steering wheel matched the one on the enormous hubcap.

Samantha smiled; then she steered her cycle in the direction of the giant tire.

"What are you doing?" Fiona called out to her.

"Wait!" Lainey shouted.

Samantha kept driving. As she got close to the wall of the pit, the sunburst on her steering wheel blinked three times. In front of her, two sections of the wall slid apart like sliding doors.

Samantha rolled straight through the open doors and into a narrow tunnel, followed by Fiona and Lainey. A paved road with a dotted white line stretched as far ahead as she could see. As she drove, overhead lights blinked on above her. She looked back to see that the lights turned off again after they passed.

Ahead, a bar stuck out from one side of the tunnel, dangling a sign above the road:

MONOWAY
ROUTE 15

Samantha smiled. The number fifteen in a circle made sense to her now. She was on her way to warn Nipper before he got stuck on track 12 for a week.

CHAPTER THIRTY-SIX

CYCLE-OLOGY

Ahead, the narrow tunnel came to an end. A dead end.

It looked like her monocycle would crash into a wall, but Samantha wasn't worried. As she got close to the wall, the sunburst on her steering wheel blinked three times, and the wall in front of her tilted back and became a ramp. She drove up and out into fresh air, followed by Lainey and Fiona.

Nearly all of the secret travel Samantha had done up to this point involved sitting, tumbling, or hanging on for dear life. For the first time as a super-secret explorer, she was in control!

She guided her electric monocycle along the path as it cut through an empty field and tried to guess their location. They were heading south and west from

Michigan. The frame of her big wheel rattled as she bounced over the choppy terrain. Fiona's monocycle whizzed up beside hers.

"I may have figured out where we are," Samantha told her. "I think we're somewhere in Indiana."

"I made the same calculation," said Fiona. "Based on wheel speed and duration, we're west of Indianapolis. Judging by current angle of the sun, forty degrees latitude seems like—"

"Okay, you win," said Samantha, laughing. "You *really* figured it out."

Fiona gave a thumbs-up, then slowed her monocycle a bit to let Samantha lead the way.

Samantha saw the sunburst on her steering wheel blinking. Ahead, another Monoway sign stood on a pole in the middle of the empty field. She pressed the brake pedal with her foot and brought her wheel to a smooth stop. Lainey and Fiona pulled up on each side of her.

Beneath the words ROUTE 15, the sign featured two arrows.

The arrow pointing to the left said ST. LOUIS. The arrow pointing to the right said CAWKER CITY.

"Which way?" Lainey asked.

"We're going to get back on the *kogelbaan* in Cawker City, Kansas," Samantha said. "That's the station that will get us home fastest. Right, Fiona?"

Fiona nodded.

"But we have to go to St. Louis first and leave a warning there for my brother," Samantha added. "That's where Nipper is going to wind up, right, Lainey?"

"Based on my knowledge of little brothers, their need for snacks, and their limited attention spans . . . yes," Lainey answered.

Samantha hit the pedal and steered in the direction of St. Louis.

After about a mile, the sunburst started blinking again. Ahead, a steel plate dropped into the earth, creating a downward ramp. Samantha sped into a new underground stretch of Monoway 15.

Her monocycle's engine hummed softly, and she cruised over smooth pavement. She could hear her friends talking behind her.

"Hey, Lainey," Fiona called. "What did the impatient little brother say when he saw a family of ducks walking in front of a—"

"Quack! Quack! Quack! Quack! Quack! Quack!" shouted Lainey. "Quack! Quack . . . quack."

Lainey had run out of breath.

"I'm the person who *invented* that joke," said Lainey.

"I suspected as much," said Fiona. "But I was curious to see how many times you could quack before you ran out of air."

As Samantha steered her monocycle, she heard her friends laughing together. She laughed a bit, too. This was the most fun she had had during her super-secret travels.

She thought of her uncle's words when they were back in Buffy's apartment: "You must be so-serious."

Did he say that because he wanted her to be serious about everything? Or was he joking that she was too serious all the time?

"I can tell you're thinking about a boy," said Lainey.

Samantha hadn't noticed Lainey pulling up beside her.

"It might be a grown-up," said Fiona, zooming up on the other side. "Possibly a teenager."

"That's right," said Lainey. "Possibly one with a motorcycle."

Samantha hadn't been thinking about a teenage boy with a motorcycle at all. But now she was! She really didn't want to tell them about Seydou or danger or super-secret trips around the world.

"Super secrets can also be used for super-evil schemes."

She wasn't sure what Uncle Paul was trying to tell her when he'd said that. But she knew he wanted her to be careful about sharing super secrets.

Samantha sped up to put some distance between her monocycle and the ones driven by *so-smart* and *so-curious*.

Monocycles

In 1869, Richard Hemming patented the "Flying Yankee Velocipede," a hand-powered single-wheel vehicle, also known as a *monowheel*. When gas engines became popular, the monocycle was born.

Monowheels and monocycles are similar to unicycles, but instead of sitting above the wheel, the rider sits inside the wheel. Inventors hoped that their vehicles' giant wheel would help them roll over rough terrain.

Unlike cars and motorcycles, however, monocycles never really caught on. As paved roads spread across the U.S., wheels taller than a person became unnecessary.

Today monocycles are considered a form of novelty motorized transportation and are mostly used for fun. No government or corporation has ever announced any form of monocycle-optimized highway network.

* * *

Monoway 15 links a dozen cities in the United States, including Allen Park, Michigan; St. Louis, Missouri; and Cawker City, Kansas. The route includes a combination of overland and underground passages.

Unlike a lot of super-secret underground travel, you won't need to bring your own lighting equipment with you. The entire Monoway is designed with environmentally friendly automatic lighting.

CHAPTER THIRTY-SEVEN

PIT STOP

Monoway 15 ended at a shallow, sunken clearing surrounded by a circle of tall bushes and short trees. Samantha heard people milling about. Above the tree line, the huge silver Gateway Arch filled the sky.

"Wait right here," said Samantha, stepping out of her monocycle.

"Can I come along?" Lainey asked. "I bet this park is crawling with little brothers, and I'd like to see if—"

"Wait here!" Samantha said again, more sternly than she meant to.

Lainey and Fiona both looked startled.

She needed to leave a clue so Nipper would find a super-secret travel spot from the Plans, but the last thing she needed was a pair of super-smart girls following her and figuring out all her super secrets.

"Sorry," she said. "I need to do this part alone."

"Okay," said Lainey. "We'll make up some new jokes while you're gone."

"Surely you're not serious," Fiona said to her.

Samantha stepped through the bushes into a quiet, grassy clearing. She glanced left and right. No one seemed to notice her. She yanked the umbrella from her shoulder, popped it open, and placed it on the ground. She pulled open her purse, fumbled through the contents, grabbed Nipper's hand lens, and . . .

She took a deep breath.

"Okay," she whispered. "I'm o-kay."

Everything was fine. She didn't mean to snap at Lainey. She just got worried that she or Fiona was going to figure out all kinds of secrets. That wasn't why she'd brought them along. Nipper needed her help, and she need their help . . . and that was it.

Samantha took another deep breath and let it out slowly. She felt much better. She sat down on the grass beside the umbrella and sighed. The sun was shining. It was a beautiful day. Not a cloud in the sky. The kind of day people dream of in Seattle. She leaned over the Super-Secret Plans, peered through the hand lens, and went to work.

She hunted around the secret map until she found a curve that looked like the Gateway Arch. The unique shape wasn't hard to find. Next to one leg of the arch there was a rectangle, and under that, a U shape looked like a smaller version of the arch, but upside down. From there, a dotted line led to the ear of corn.

She smiled with satisfaction. She had planned this out when she had studied the Plans earlier. They had reached the middle of her super-secret shortcut.

Samantha stood up and closed the umbrella. Then she put Nipper's hand lens in her purse and stepped between the bushes on the other side of the clearing. She hurried across the field and joined the path leading to the Gateway Arch, pushing past several crowds along the way.

She gazed at the base of the monument in the distance, then marched up to a spot that didn't look like anything special. She squinted at it and saw the faint outline of a rectangle. She might not have noticed it at all if Fiona hadn't showed her how to spot the secret door by the *kogelbaan* station under Seattle.

Samantha opened her purse and took out the old gum Lainey had scraped off the floor in Seattle. She estimated Nipper's height and stuck it onto the arch at his eye level. Then she walked back to the clearing.

She could see her friends waiting for her on their monocycles, and she made her way back to them.

"Ready to go?" she asked.

Both girls nodded and started their engines.

Samantha hopped into her big wheel and started her engine, too. She pressed the gas pedal and took off across the shallow, sunken clearing and accelerated down into Monoway 15.

The three monocycles hummed and rolled through tunnels and over prairies, heading back to the *kogelbaan*.

Samantha started thinking about how Fiona and Lainey had helped her find and mark the secret door without even knowing it.

"Don't worry, Sam," said Lainey, riding up next to her. "I'm not mad at you. People who have little brothers sometimes get annoyed and sound crosser than they mean to."

Samantha nodded. Lainey was sure right about that one. She didn't say anything, however. She was too busy thinking about her super-annoying little brother. She steered her monocycle straight ahead, hoping Nipper would see her secret sticky clue.

CHAPTER THIRTY-EIGHT

ON GUARD

Auguste Goulot clutched the leather-wrapped handle of his opera glasses with one hand and adjusted the digital controls with the other. With a flick of his thumb, he increased the magnification from 10x to 40x. He pressed them close to the long narrow window of the Gateway Arch observatory deck.

This was a fine spot to view the park and the surrounding city. Goulot watched carefully. He didn't want to miss anything. He was almost out of cities.

In the three months since he arrived in the United States, Goulot crisscrossed the country, visiting landmark after landmark in town after town. From Boston to Las Vegas, he searched. From there, he went to Atlanta, and on to Houston. Now, as he stood high over the streets of St. Louis, Missouri, he knew it was only one of two cities left.

He glanced down at the worn, marked-up map in his hands, and then looked out the window again. He admired the shadow of the Gateway Arch stretching over the park below. What a marvelous monument. A thing of beauty, a masterpiece of engineering, and the tallest building in the city. It reminded him of his beloved Tour Eiffel.

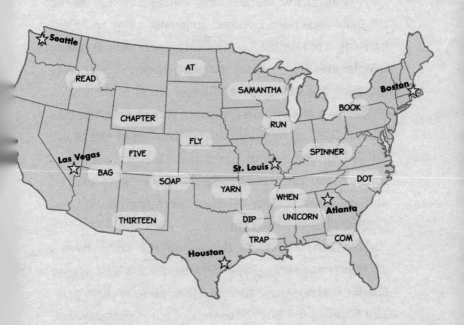

The Eiffel Tower, where he was once a security guard. It was the best job he ever had. He loved greeting visitors from around the world. He delighted in telling people facts about the tower and all kinds of things about Paris. Then those mysterious kids ruined everything!

On a sunny Saturday last April, Détective Auguste Goulot, assistant director of Eiffel Tower security, took his usual lunch break, strolling the path along the river Seine. Suddenly he heard someone shout for help. He raced to investigate.

A Pain du Jour bicycle cart whizzed by him in the opposite direction. Two kids followed: a boy and a girl carrying a red umbrella. A minute later, several smelly people dressed in black pursued them. It was very alarming and strange. He followed them to the tower.

But two of them disappeared! Apparently, the kids who dashed up to the first-level landing of the tower ducked around a steel beam and vanished without a trace. Many tourists around the tower were excited and confused. A few of them were frightened. And Goulot's boss . . . was furious!

Hundreds of people flowed up the stairs to see what was happening, and because Détective Auguste Goulot was not there to stop them, none of them paid. The Eiffel Tower lost thousands of euros that day, and Goulot lost his job.

But he would set things right. He would find those two kids. He had made a vow to the moon and stars! He would bring them to justice, and he would return to Paris as a triumphant crime stopper!

He removed his special Eiffel Tower–shaped badge, polished it on his sleeve, and pinned it back on his coat. Then something caught his eye.

Far below, a girl marched through the crowds and directly up to a leg of the Gateway Arch. She touched the arch and then marched away.

Goulot increased the magnification to 75x. The girl carried a red umbrella! He continued watching.

The girl walked to a clearing beyond the park. Two other people waited for her. The three of them drove away on large one-wheeled vehicles.

Goulot recognized the machines immediately. He could name 763 different types of vehicles. These were *monocycles.*

The three wheels plunged behind a cluster of trees . . . and vanished. Completely!

He raised his map and began to study it again.

The monocycles were headed in a northwesterly direction. He felt certain that they were heading to the only city left on his map: Seattle, the Emerald City.

"La Ville Émeraude," he said to himself, and smiled.

CHAPTER THIRTY-NINE

BACK ON TRACK

The three girls cruised side by side from eastern Missouri to central Kansas. Samantha rode in silence, enjoying the scenery. Then . . .

"Waitaminute!" Lainey shouted, and pulled ahead of the pack.

She brought her monocycle to a stop beside a sign that read:

WELCOME TO CAWKER CITY

Samantha caught up with her and stopped. She noticed that Lainey's face was lit up with excitement.

"The world's biggest ball of twine is in this town," Lainey told her. "If I had a little brother with me, I know the first thing he'd want to do would be to—"

"But *you* don't have a little brother with you," Fiona interrupted as she rolled up beside them. "You don't have a little brother yourself at all. Do you?"

Lainey didn't answer. She looked straight ahead past Fiona.

Samantha thought her expression was angry or sad until she realized Lainey was staring at a bus stop along a road a few yards away.

"Boy in the ball?" asked Samantha.

"Possibly," said Lainey.

"Definitely," said Fiona, squinting in the same direction.

"Wow," said Samantha. "You sure have keen eyesight."

"It comes in handy," said Fiona, looking up at the sky.

Samantha could tell she was calculating the position of the sun.

"It's after two right now in Kansas," Fiona continued. "We'll get two hours back in Washington State because of the time zone difference. If we head home without stopping, we should all make it by dinner."

Samantha hit the gas and led the way. In about a hundred yards, they reached another round, sunken clearing. It was much smaller than the pit by the giant tire in Michigan, but it was still a circle hidden in plain sight.

They parked their monocycles, and from there, they walked back to the bus stop marked with the boy in the ball and found a staircase hidden from view behind a power transformer.

Five minutes later, they were sitting packed tightly together on a foam couch, in a ball on the *kogelbaan*, rolling home.

The Uniroyal Giant Tire

An enormous tire looms beside a stretch of highway near Allen Park, Michigan.

Originally, the giant tire was a Ferris wheel, built by the United States Rubber Company for the 1964 New York World's Fair. More than two million people rode in baskets around the outside of the tire. When the fair ended, the owners disassembled it and shipped it to Michigan, where it became an advertisement for Uniroyal Tires.

At over eighty feet high, it is the largest tire ever built and one of the largest roadside attractions in the United States.

The World's Biggest Ball of Twine

In Cawker City, Kansas, a giant twine ball rests under a small shelter.

While many others have claimed to create the "world's biggest" balls of twine, string, or yarn, at fourteen feet, two and a half inches, the ball in Kansas is the official record holder for all three types. It contains about 1,500 miles of string and weighs an estimated twenty thousand pounds.

Visitors to Cawker City are welcome to stop by and add to the ball anytime. Appointments are recommended.

* * *

Both the giant tire and the world's biggest ball of twine are located near *two* super-secret travel systems. They are both close to stations for track 12 of the *kogelbaan* and near Monoway 15. If you need to skip part of the *kogelbaan*, get off at Allen Park and take a monocycle shortcut. You can rejoin the *kogelbaan* in Kansas.

If you want to get farther along track 12 than the station in Kansas, drive your monocycle to Mitchell, South Dakota. There you'll find three super-secret travel systems: the *kogelbaan*, the Monoway, and the hoverdisk highway.

CHAPTER FORTY

FELL-EVATOR

Nipper sat near the back of the bus as he rode from Collinsville, Illinois, to St. Louis, Missouri. The marble coaster had been a ton of fun. For a long time. Then it became not-so-fun. Then it was really boring.

When Nipper first left the ball station, he wasn't sure where to go. He tried hard to figure out what Samantha would do. Then he saw a billboard for the Gateway Arch in nearby St. Louis. That huge silver arch had to be the tallest thing in the city. If Sam was going to leave him a super-secret clue, that was where he should look.

At first, the bus driver didn't want to accept the old silver dollar Nipper had in his pocket. Eventually, the man agreed to take it. Now Nipper sat in his seat, watching the arch grow bigger as they approached. His hands rested on the seat back in front of him.

He noticed a bit of yellow yarn on his wrist. It made him think of mustard . . . and hamburgers. His stomach rumbled, so he turned and looked out the window. On the side of the road he saw . . . a giant bottle of ketchup! It made him think of French fries.

"Enough," said Nipper.

He reached into his pocket and pulled out a fistful of marshmallow circus peanuts. He bit one and chewed. It had almost no flavor. He swallowed and took another bite. Awful. Sad.

"These are terrible," he said.

He chewed and swallowed. Then he counted the orange candy peanuts in his hand.

"And I have so few of them," he added, putting the rest back in his pocket.

Ten minutes later, Nipper filed off the bus with the other passengers. This was definitely a major attraction. Tourists milled about. A few feet away stood a man in a green T-shirt. A camera with a large lens hung from a strap around his neck. He spoke to a much older woman, a teenage girl, and a toddler. They wore matching green T-shirts with the words *Family Reunions Du Jour.*

". . . *la estructura mas alta,*" the man was saying to the group.

That sounded familiar. Uncle Paul had spent a ton of time teaching Samantha how to say "Where's the tallest building?" in eleven languages. Nipper paid attention occasionally. He was pretty sure the man in the green T-shirt spoke Spanish.

"Welcome to the USA," said Nipper cheerfully.

The man looked confused. Then he smiled.

"No welcome needed," the man said. "We're from Detroit, Michigan. I was just talking to my mother in Spanish," he explained. "She was born in Mexico. We speak Spanish and English at home."

Nipper shrugged. That made sense to him.

The man looked at his family again and back to Nipper.

"Would you mind?" said the man, removing the camera and holding it out.

"Sure," said Nipper, taking it from him.

The family bunched together so there was a clear view of the stainless steel arch behind them, and they all smiled.

"Say cheese," said Nipper.

"Cheese!" they all said.

Nipper was about to snap a photo, but he started thinking about cheese. His stomach rumbled. He sure was hungry.

He centered the family in the big camera's viewfinder again, and something caught his eye on the side of the arch behind the family.

Nipper squinted at the wall behind them.

"*Rápidamente, por favor,*" said the grandmother.

"Oh, right. Sorry," he said, and snapped several pictures.

"*Gracias,*" said the man, taking back his camera.

"*De nada,*" Nipper replied.

He had learned to say "you're welcome" in Spanish from Samantha when she was preparing for their trip to Peru.

Nipper waited until the family had moved on and went to investigate the mystery spot.

He stepped over the hedge lining the sidewalk and walked up to the side of the arch. There was a dark spot on the shiny stainless steel surface, exactly at his eye level. It could be a coincidence. Or maybe someone who knew him put it there. He moved closer and reached the wall to see . . . a wad of gum.

He tapped at it. He smelled his finger. Then he pulled it off the wall and gave it a good sniff. It smelled like grape. It was the gum from the big machine room under Seattle!

"Thanks, Sam," he said quietly, and began to search the wall of the arch in front of him.

At first, Nipper didn't see anything special, just the smooth silvery surface. Then he took a closer look at the wall. Ever so faintly, he noticed the thin outline of a rectangle. He touched his finger to his lips as he tried to think. He tasted grape. The wad of gum was still stuck to his finger. He shoved the blob into his pocket and went back to staring at the wall.

"What would Samantha do?" he said softly.

He pictured the horse statue in Italy, the one he activated by sticking a finger in its nose. That was awesome, but there was no nose to pick here.

Nipper thought about the fake stupa dome in Indonesia. That turned out to be a balloon. He pressed against the side of the Gateway Arch. Nope. This thing was solid.

Then he thought about the secret sliding panel that he and Samantha discovered at Machu Picchu. He put his hand back on the side of the arch . . . and smiled. He pressed hard, and a rectangular section panel slid sideways.

"Gotcha," said Nipper.

There was a secret room inside! He looked left and right. He was pretty sure that was what Samantha would do. Then his stomach rumbled. He stepped into the arch. Lined with wood paneling, it looked a lot like an elevator. Across from the entrance, in the center of the wall, a button blinked. It had a glowing letter D on it.

Things didn't seem right. He wanted to go *up* to the top of the arch. What could D mean?

"Down? Dip? Dive?" Nipper puzzled. "Descend? Drop? Dump?"

But it was a big glowing button. He felt drawn to it.

He couldn't think of any "up" words that started with the letter D.

It didn't matter. It was a glowing, blinking button.

He pressed it.

Behind Nipper's back, the door slammed shut, and the floor opened up beneath him. The walls of the room zoomed up and out of sight as he dropped like a giant steel marble.

"*Yaaaaaaaaaaaaaaaaaaaaaaaaaaaaaaaaaaaaaah!*" he screamed as he plunged into darkness. "*Yaaaaaaaaaaaaa aaaaaaaaaaaaaaaaaaaaaaaaaaaaaaaah! Yaaaaaaaaaaa—*"

CHAPTER FORTY-ONE

BACK AND FOURTH

"—aaaaaaaaaaaaaaaaaaaaaaaaaaaah!" Nipper shouted. "Yaaaaaaaaaaaah!"

He fell and fell.

In total darkness, he dropped farther and farther into an endless pit.

Suddenly he brushed against a wall. He brushed again and again. Then the wall seemed to shift toward him. He bumped it. And bumped it again and again . . . and then he was sliding! The wall had curved under him.

Feetfirst, Nipper slid like a rocket through the darkness—a rocket on the world's longest playground slide. Up ahead, a dot of light appeared. It grew closer and closer and—Nipper whizzed past it!

Immediately the slide curved upward. The light disappeared behind him as he rose higher and higher—and stopped.

"Waitaminute! Waitaminute!" Nipper screamed.

He began to drop. Now he was sliding backward.

He zoomed headfirst, until the surface beneath him curved again. The light sped past him, and then he was rising, headfirst.

Seconds later, he stopped and slid downward. He blew past the light and whizzed upward once more.

"I've got it!" Nipper shouted. "This is an upside-down arch!"

He slid past the light and up, then down past the light in the other direction.

This time, he skidded to a stop. Light streamed in from an opening to one side of the underground arch.

Nipper stood up and rubbed his shoulder. Then he looked down and began to search.

"Aha," he said, and picked up several orange candy peanuts and shoved them back into his pocket. Falling on the ground couldn't hurt them.

Nipper was about to walk through the opening and into the light when he heard rumbling. Above, in the darkness, someone else was cruising down the arch.

"Sam!" he called upward. "Is that you?"

The noise grew louder. Nipper was pretty sure it was more than one person, bumping and sliding. It might be three people.

One by one, *four* white figures zoomed past Nipper. They disappeared. Then came skidding back in from the other side and stopped and climbed to their feet.

Two men and two women stood in front of Nipper. Each wore a long white coat and bright white sneakers. One of the women stepped forward.

Nipper glanced at some writing stitched to her front left pocket:

$$a^2 + b^2 = c^2$$

"Mister Spinner?" she said.

There was something sinister in the way the woman asked that, and, besides, Nipper could tell it wasn't really a question.

Nipper studied the numbers on the woman's pocket again.

"A squared plus b squared," he said carefully.

She watched him, suspiciously.

"Calcu . . . later!" Nipper shouted, and dashed between the four strangers.

CHAPTER FORTY-TWO

ARCH ENEMIES

Nipper charged through the doorway, turned left, and headed down a long ramp.

"Who were those guys?" he said to himself as he ran.

At the bottom of the ramp, the floor changed from gray to white.

"Waitaminute waitaminute," said Nipper, stopping just before he reached the different-colored floor.

The floor was hissing!

He stuck out one foot and lowered it onto the white surface. His foot slipped forward, and he pulled it back.

He crouched and held his hand an inch above the floor. Tiny jets of air pushed against his palm. It was like an air hockey table.

He glanced sideways. A row of big white disks leaned against one wall. Each one was the size of an extra-large pizza.

Nipper started thinking about extra-large pizzas with double cheese, pepperoni, and just one anchovy that he would try to trick his sister into biting.

"Stop!" a voice shouted. "You're wanted for *trigonome-treason!*"

He looked back and saw the strangers marching down the ramp. He had only one chance to get out of there. He grabbed one of the disks. It was thick plastic. He tossed it onto the white surface, gave himself a running start, and leaped.

Nipper shot forward, riding the disk like an air hockey puck!

Overhead hung a purple sign with bright orange letters and numbers.

HOVERDISK HIGHWAY
MAXIMUM SPEED: 400 MPH

Nipper shifted his weight to keep his balance on the disk. Then he leaned forward, just a bit, and really took off!

Wind whipped at his hair as he sped through the tunnel. He had no idea how fast he was going . . . but it was definitely fast.

Gradually he figured out how to control the disk. He leaned a little to the left and then to the right. His disk swerved left and right on the highway.

"Trigonome-treason?" Nipper pondered.

It sounded familiar. It sounded like trigonometry. It sounded like . . . *trigonometry time trials*! They must be from calculus camp!

"Young man!" shouted someone behind him. "Reverse your x-axis!"

Nipper didn't want to be captured by math police from Camp Pythagoras. He didn't want to pantomime story problems, go fraction foraging, or do square root ceramics!

He glanced back quickly and saw the four figures in white, coasting after him.

Nipper had just survived a giant yarn ball, a power dryer, a ninja monkey, a marble disaster, and two strangers with jumpsuits and helmets. There was no way he was going to do math problems.

He leaned forward and accelerated.

CHAPTER FORTY-THREE

SURF'S UP

Swish!

Something shiny and silver sailed over Nipper's head, missing it by a fraction of an inch.

"Good thing I'm not Sam," he said, touching a spot on his forehead. "That would have hit her right here."

He shielded his eyes and looked back. The math police were coasting behind him. Each one stood on a disk, racing along. The one closest to him raised a hand. She held up a shiny silver protractor that twinkled under the spotlights of the hoverdisk highway. She moved her hand back and forth, as if calculating the best angle for throwing it.

Nipper used one hand to keep his balance on the speeding disk. He reached up and felt his head where the first protractor had grazed him. A chunk of hair was gone.

Swish!

The second protractor sailed past his face, barely missing his nose.

"I hate math!" he shouted, and leaned forward to make the disk move even faster.

In the distance, a sign dangled from the ceiling. Dark purple letters against an orange background:

WARNING!

CLEARANCE = 1.3 FEET

He looked over his shoulder. The math police were still behind him. He faced forward to see the rapidly approaching sign again . . . and smiled.

Nipper reached into his pocket and pulled out the wad of grape gum. It stuck to one of the candy peanuts.

The sign grew closer.

Nipper checked the gum on the back of the candy for stickiness. It was still good and sticky. He reached up and slapped the gum onto the sign as he coasted beneath it. Then he lay forward and made himself as flat on the disk as he possibly could.

CHAPTER FORTY-FOUR

PROS AND CON-CUSSIONS

"I can still see him!" shouted Agent $a^2 + b^2 = c^2$.

She shifted her weight, bringing her hoverdisk to an optimal fifteen-degree angle above the floor of the tunnel. Steadily she gained speed.

The other three Super Numerical Overachievers zoomed behind her along the hoverdisk highway. Using a combination of balance, quick reflexes, and precise computation, they closed in on the boy.

Up ahead, a sign displayed purple letters against an orange background:

WARNING!

CLEARANCE = 1 3 FEET

"Why is there a warning when the clearance is thirteen feet?" asked Agent $ax^2 + bx + c$.

"That's a very good question," noted Agent 3.1415.

"Stop jabbering, and keep your eyes on that annoying boy," yelled Agent $E^{in} + 1 = 0$. "The sooner we catch him, the sooner we can—"

Wham!

Wham!

Wham!

Wham!

The four Super Numerical Overachievers slammed into a horizontally extending beam, exactly 1.3 feet above the tunnel floor.

CHAPTER FORTY-FIVE

A CHANGE OF HEART

Nipper glided along on his disk, staying as low as he could. Horizontal beams whizzed overhead. Each time he passed under one, he felt a new blast of air. When the gusts stopped, he looked up. The space above him was clear again.

He glanced over his shoulder. Behind him were four hoverdisks—with nobody riding on them. All four of the math police were gone!

"The number thirteen turned out to be good luck this time," he said.

He stood up on the disk and coasted. Wind whipped at his hair.

"Okay," he told himself. "Maybe I don't hate math after all."

Nipper kept his balance, but he started to relax.

"For now, anyway," he added.

Ahead, the color of the floor changed from white to gray.

Nipper thought about his dad . . . and math. His dad used math to do some pretty cool tricks.

His hoverdisk skidded to a stop.

Come to think of it, his dad could do a ton of amazing things. Both his parents could. And they never got chased by ninjas, clowns, or monkeys.

He spotted a staircase leading to an open door. Sunlight streamed in from above.

"You know," said Nipper, "maybe it's time to grow up a little. This could be the start of a whole new formula. I could make big changes in my life."

As he stood there, an expression of wonder crept across his face.

"I *could* take a bath every few days. Maybe I'll start wearing clean socks," he said.

Nipper picked a strand of yarn from his shirt.

"I *could* pay more attention to my surroundings," he said, getting excited. "Maybe I won't break everything in the house quite as often. I might not lose as much stuff. I could even try to be less annoying."

He took a deep breath and thought about it for a minute.

"Naaaaaaaah!" he said.

He pulled a circus peanut from his pocket.

"But I am willing to give these candies another try," he said.

Nipper popped it into his mouth and chewed. Then he marched up the stairs, looking for another circle with a picture of a boy in the center.

CHAPTER FORTY-SIX

CRASH COURSE

Crash Nitro finally had a moment to herself. She removed her helmet and let her hair tumble to her shoulders. She reached into one of the deep pockets of her jumpsuit, pulled out a brush, and began to stroke her long locks of red, orange, yellow, and green. And blue and indigo. And violet.

It used to be so much easier, back in Australia. As the notorious Rainbow Thief, she struck terror into the hearts of jewelers, art collectors, and bankers alike. No museum was safe from the Rainbow Thief. No alarm system too clever.

Her brush caught in a snarl.

"Stupid motorcycle helmet," she grumbled.

She had been too successful. Word had spread about the amazing acrobatic thief with the rainbow hair. Everyone was on the lookout. Stealing became more difficult, and she couldn't spend any loot without being identified. She had two choices: cut her hair or leave Australia. She left, of course.

She tugged and pulled the brush through her glorious mane. Yes, she had come up with a fine scam. The goofy daredevils did her bidding and handed over stolen goods without asking any questions. And all she had to do was pass around a little candy every now and then.

Crash Nitro heard footsteps approaching. She quickly put her helmet on and stuffed her hair into her collar.

Three daredevils scrambled into the room. She had no idea which ones. She never bothered to remember the names she gave them.

"I hope there's a reason you're interrupting my planning time," said Crash Nitro.

Ever since that ninja told Crash Nitro about the amazing map-umbrella, she'd spent hours every day obsessed with the idea of owning it. With a super-secret map, she could finally go back to Australia. She could be the Rainbow Thief again, and no one would be able to catch her!

For weeks, Crash Nitro had told daredevils to be on the lookout for a girl with a red umbrella. She thought the girl was from Seattle. Then some clowns said they saw the same girl in Florence, Italy. Other clowns said they spotted the girl and umbrella in Mopti, Mali. The girl was everywhere.

"So," said Crash Nitro, "has someone spotted the umbrella again?"

"Nope," said the daredevil. "But there's a boy on a ball!"

"What?" asked Crash Nitro.

"There's an amazing boy on a ball!" a second daredevil said excitedly.

"*On* a ball?" asked Crash Nitro.

"Yeah," said the second daredevil. "He rode on top while fighting a ninja monkey!"

"At first we thought he was going to be super annoying," said the third daredevil. "But it was an unstoppable stunt!"

"Waitaminute, waitaminute, waitaminute," said Crash Nitro.

She pulled the photo from her pocket and stared at the boy running beside the girl with the umbrella. He looked annoying. Super annoying.

"Bring me that boy," she said quickly. "Grab him. Use a net. Hit him with pool noodles. I don't care. Get him here."

She unzipped her fanny pack and picked through the contents.

"The first CLOUD who captures the boy . . . gets this!"

She held up a flimsy plastic ring. It had a green rubber scorpion on top.

"Holy cow!" said the first daredevil.

Crash Nitro pressed down on the top of the ring. The scorpion started blinking.

"Whoa, Nelly!" said the second daredevil. "I just *love* things that blink. I don't know why."

"A toy!" they all shouted. "A cool toy!"

"Eee-NUFF!" she hollered.

They quieted down instantly.

"Any questions?" Crash Nitro said calmly.

A daredevil raised her hand.

"Scorpions have eight legs," she said.

"That's not a question!" she barked. "Bring me that boy now!"

"Catch the boy . . . get a toy!" the daredevils chanted. "Catch the boy . . . get a toy!"

The Space Needle

Just north of downtown Seattle, a celebrated landmark rises above the city streets. It looks like a flying saucer on stilts.

Since it opened in 1962, more than sixty million people have ridden to the top for a breathtaking view of the city, the mountains, and Puget Sound—when the weather is clear, of course.

At 605 feet, it is not the tallest building in the city. However, it is the structure that almost always comes to mind first when people think of the Emerald City.

The Elephant Car Wash

Just a few blocks from the Space Needle, a large pink sign shaped like an elephant turns slowly above the street.

   While not nearly as tall or as famous as the Space Needle, the Elephant Car Wash sign is still a beloved landmark to many people who live in Seattle. When most people spot the happy neon elephant, it makes them smile.

* * *

An underground chamber, located halfway between these two treasures, is the lair of Clandestine League of Unstoppable Daredevils, aka the CLOUD.

Originally, they were a loosely organized band of talented yet undisciplined skateboarders, acrobats, and trampoline artists. Recently, however, they have fallen under the control of a criminal leader from Australia. They now use their skills to perform jewelry heists and art gallery robberies in exchange for . . . candy.

CHAPTER FORTY-SEVEN

LOST AND HOUND

George Spinner sat in the center seat of the H-shaped vehicle. What an amazing underground network of magnetically levitating trains! In a single day, he and his brother had traveled to and from Paris, Edfu, Wahoo, Duck, and Baraboo. Remarkable.

They hadn't found Nipper, but maybe this next trip would lead them to the boy. George had heard of Wagga Wagga, Australia. It sounded like a funny place. Now he could visit and find out for himself.

"I'm coming." Paul's voice echoed through the hall from the Baraboo magtrain station.

George smiled. He waited eagerly to press the orange button again. With almost no friction, they'd zoom back to Seattle at thousands of miles per hour.

At first, traveling together had been difficult. They were so different. But little by little, they found ways to cooperate. His older brother, Paul, loved to explore and was fantastic at figuring out secret clues and learning new languages.

George, of course, had a passion for science and math. He was a master of useless facts, and every now and then, he would be called upon to use his special talents.

Paul didn't seem to be as focused on finding Nipper as George had expected. He actually got the feeling that his brother was just keeping both of them busy while Samantha was out tracking down Nipper. It didn't make sense, but he hoped his brother would show him more super-secret transportation systems.

"Let's visit one more magtrain station," said Paul, climbing into the backseat of the train car. "If we don't see Nipper there, I'll take you to the conservatory in Volunteer Park. I'll show you how to ride the slide—"

Paul froze. His eyes darted around the train car.

"Where's the dog?" he asked quickly.

"I thought he was with you," George replied.

Bzzt-zzzt-zzzzt. Zzzz-zzzz-zzzzzzt!

His shoes buzzed extra loud.

Paul winced. He covered his ears with his hands and made one of his more irritated faces.

"Why are they so loud?" he asked.

"I turned them up to full power," said George. "In case the boy is really far away."

Bzzt-zzzt-zzzzt. Zzzz-zzzz-zzzzzzt!

"Then again," George continued, "this might be painful . . . for the delicate ears . . . of a . . ."

George didn't finish the sentence. It was clear that his brother knew the next word was going to be *dog*.

"I'm changing the plan," said Paul. "As soon as we reach Wagga Wagga, we're turning around and heading home."

"Home?" said George.

"Yes," said his brother. "And you're going to call Suzette . . . right now."

CHAPTER FORTY-EIGHT

GONE IN SIXTY SANDALS

Pango-lango-lango-langolin! Pango-lango-lango-langolin!

Dr. Suzette Spinner steered the massive flatbed truck over to the shoulder of Interstate 90. She used her turn signals and braked slowly, making sure all of the Dazzling Dozen stopped safely behind her. Then she opened the glove compartment and grabbed her phone.

"Hi, George," she answered.

"Hi, Suzette," said her husband. "I have something very important to tell you."

She waited.

"But first . . . ," George said slowly. "How is the drive?"

"The drive is fine, dear," she replied. "Steering a massive eighteen-wheeled truck isn't as tricky as I thought it would be. What's so important?"

"How is Buffy?" asked George.

"Well . . . actually, she's gone," said Dr. Spinner. "She flew back to California. She told me she really wanted to be back at school."

"Really?" he replied. "Since when?"

"Since I gave her that lecture about the importance of education," said Suzette. "I did it over and over again. Then, suddenly Buffy got really excited. She demanded that I take her to an airport."

"Interesting," said George.

"She grabbed her favorite thirty pairs of shoes, and then I dropped her off at the Municipal Airport outside of Mitchell, South Dakota," Suzette explained.

"How did you get her to change her mind?" asked George.

"I'm not exactly sure," she answered truthfully.

"If I remember correctly, Buffy only listens to every thirteenth word you tell her," said George. "Maybe you should review the exact words you used in that lecture. Maybe there's a clue. . . ."

She waited. She could tell her husband was doing some kind of calculation or puzzle in his head. Of course, he was almost always doing that.

"I'll see you Sunday," she said.

"Kisses," he replied.

Suzette smiled.

"Wait," she said. "Wasn't there something important you wanted to tell me?"

Her husband had already hung up.

CHAPTER FORTY-NINE

OF DOGS AND SHOES

George sat next to his brother on the magtrain as they zoomed home from Wagga Wagga.

"I forgot to tell Suzette about Nipper," he said.

"I know," said Paul.

The breeze whipped at his hair.

"I forgot to tell her about Dennis, too," said George.

"I know," said Paul.

They sat silently in the speeding magtrain car for a while.

George looked to his right. His brother had that mysterious look on his face. He always wore that expression.

"Sounds can also unlock powerful memories," said George.

"True," said Paul.

The walls of the tunnel whizzed by. The train raced along at more than ten thousand miles per hour.

"You know what I think?" asked George.

"What's that?" asked Paul.

"I think the sounds from these dog clogs—or even just the *idea* of these clogs—bothers you because they make you remember our dog Button."

"That was a long time ago," said Paul.

"I know," said George. "Thirty-eight years ago."

The train zipped onward.

"You know what?" asked George.

"What?" asked Paul.

"*Lo siento,*" said George.

"What?" asked Paul.

"*Je suis désolé,*" said George.

"That's pretty good," said Paul. "You almost pronounced the—"

"Paul," said George. "I'm sorry Button ran away. I'm really sorry."

His brother didn't say anything for a long time. The wind in the tunnel whipped at his hair.

"Thank you," he said finally.

They rode along in silence for another full minute.

"I have a theory," said George.

"What's that?" said Paul.

"I think you brought me on this adventure to give Samantha time to find Nipper," he answered.

Paul tilted his head to one side and raised an eyebrow.

"Not all by herself," he said.

"I know," said George. "But I think we've been traveling to the middle of nowhere because you want Samantha to learn some things on her own."

Paul looked straight ahead again, but George thought he could see a trace of a smile on his brother's face.

"No place is in the middle of nowhere," said Paul.

"Of course," said George.

The lights of the Seattle magtrain station were approaching.

"The Emerald City," they both said at the same time.

CHAPTER FIFTY

PARTY PLANNERS

Crash Nitro relaxed, brushing her hair.

"Red . . . orange . . . yellow . . . ," she sighed. "Green . . . blue . . . indi—"

She hit a snarl.

"Horrible helmet," she grumbled.

As soon as she got her hands on the red umbrella, she was out of here. Nothing would ever snarl her hair again. Horrible helmet . . . bye-bye. Soggy Seattle . . . bye-bye. Goofy daredevils . . . bye-bye.

She heard approaching sneakers thumping on cement. She grabbed the helmet, stuffing her hair inside, and pulled it onto her head, just in time.

A dozen daredevils scampered into the room.

"He's on his way!" one of them shouted.

"Who is?" asked Crash Nitro.

"The boy on the ball!" shouted another. "We spotted him by the Corn Palace, and we left a trail of candy. He followed it right into the ball station and rolled back to Seattle. He been following our candy trail around the station for twenty minutes."

"He must really be hungry," said a daredevil.

"It's a good thing we saved some of our best candy for him," said another.

"Wonderful," said Crash Nitro.

She rubbed her gloved hands together. Her plan was coming together nicely.

"Catch the boy . . . trap the girl," she said quietly. And even more softly, "Take the umbrella . . . ditch the CLOUD."

"What's that, boss?" said one of the daredevils.

"Nothing, nothing," said Crash Nitro.

She stood up and addressed the CLOUD.

"Spread the word, everyone," she barked. "When the boy finally gets here, we're going to throw a party."

The daredevils looked at each other, confused. Confused but also excited. Crash Nitro heard the word *party* go by in a whisper several times.

"Yes, yes," said Crash Nitro. "We'll throw the greatest celebration that the Clandestine League of Unstoppable Daredevils has ever seen."

She paced back and forth, pleased with herself. She looked up. The daredevils watched her, still confused.

"Do you see?" she asked. "We're going to keep the boy here until his sister arrives. She's the girl with the umbrella."

Crash Nitro could tell that most of the CLOUD was still having trouble with her plan. The sooner she could escape these goofballs, the better. She took a deep breath and let it out.

"Just do what I tell you," she said in a fake-friendly voice. "We'll keep the boy at the party. We'll take the umbrella. Then I'll . . . I mean, then *we'll* plan our next move."

"What if the boy doesn't want to stay?" asked a daredevil.

Crash Nitro smiled.

"Oh, he'll stay all right," she answered. "He'll stay as long as I want him to."

She walked quickly to a corner of the room.

"In case of an emergency, I've been saving . . . this!"

Dramatically, she pulled back the curtain to reveal a silver contraption about five feet tall. She flipped a switch and a six-tier chocolate fountain bubbled to life.

"*Oooo! Whoa!*" murmured the daredevils.

"Eee-NUFF!" barked Crash Nitro.

The CLOUD quieted down.

"No eight-year-old boy can resist a chocolate fountain," she explained. "It's like a knock-knock joke. He won't be able to stop himself, and he won't notice anything else that's going on."

She pulled a shiny, sharp boomerang from her pocket.

"And when the sister comes to take him home, we'll have a *pointed discussion*," she said, waving the boomerang in her gloved hand. "She can keep her umbrella—or her head."

A few of the daredevils looked worried.

Crash Nitro cleared her throat.

"Just bring the boy to the party and let the chocolate work its magic," she said, fake-sweetly. "Any questions?"

A daredevil raised her hand.

"I love chocolate fountains, too," she said.

"That's not a question!" barked Crash Nitro.

She pictured herself far, far away from Seattle, with flowing rainbow hair. Stealing anything she wanted from anyone she chose to and using the umbrella to escape. Again and again and again.

CHAPTER FIFTY-ONE

A SPLIT DECISION

Samantha turned the handle, and the giant ball came to a halt. She opened the door and stepped onto the platform. She looked up at the sign:

UITGANG:
SEATTLE

Fiona and Lainey climbed out of the ball, too. Lainey pushed the door shut. Immediately the ball rolled down the track and disappeared through a tunnel.

"Thanks," said Samantha. "Thanks for everything and all of your help today. Both of you."

"I'm not sure we did that much," said Lainey.

"Oh, but you did," said Samantha. "You helped me find clues and track Nipper. You stopped me from getting stuck inside a ball for over a week."

"Yeah," said Lainey. "That was close."

"And we did it as a team," Samantha continued. "This is the first time I've worked on a team like this. You are both amazing in completely different ways, and we put all our talents together."

"True," said Fiona. "But your brother's still missing."

"Oh, I'm going to find him," said Samantha. "Don't worry."

"Don't you want us to come with you?" asked Lainey.

"No," Samantha answered. "You've got to get home for dinner, and I'm sure Fiona has something else that needs her attention."

"True," said Fiona again.

Even if they could stick with her, Samantha wasn't sure that was a good idea. They'd had a great day together. Lainey and Fiona seemed like real—not just sort-of, kind-of—friends. But there were so many super secrets. Samantha knew she had a lot to learn about protecting them and about sharing them.

"I'll walk you out of here," she said.

They started up the stairs.

Samantha sniffed.

"Do you smell something?" she asked.

Lainey and Fiona sniffed.

"Chocolate," said Fiona, cupping a hand behind one ear. "It sounds like it's flowing down, going into a pump, and then flowing down again. Over and over."

"That's a chocolate fondue fountain," said Lainey confidently. "They had one at my neighbor's quince-añera, and all the boys went nuts."

"Not just the little brothers?" asked Fiona.

"*All* the boys went berserk. Some girls, too," said Fiona. "They kept dipping and dipping. Some people can't stop themselves. It's a lot like a knock-knock joke."

Samantha smiled. She had a pretty good sense of how Nipper would react to a chocolate fountain. Whoever put one nearby had no idea what they were in for.

The girls walked up the stairs, pushed open a door, and stepped out onto the sidewalk on Denny Way, close to the car wash.

As soon as they passed through the door, it swung shut. Samantha looked back. There was no handle. If she wanted to get back in, she'd have to return to the car wash and head down the slide again.

"I guess this is it for now," she said.

"Sure," said Fiona.

Fiona looked at the car wash, then back to Samantha.

"I hope you find . . . your little brother," said Lainey.

Then she turned and started walking.

Samantha wasn't expecting a big goodbye, but Lainey seemed subdued just then, maybe a little sad. She watched as Lainey headed up the hill.

"Well," said Fiona, "today was certainly interesting."

Samantha turned back to face her.

"I wouldn't mind coming back and investigating this in the future," Fiona added.

"Great," said Samantha. "How about next week?"

Fiona took a small notebook out of her pocket.

"Let's see," she said, flipping through it.

Samantha waited as Fiona turned pages.

"No, that won't work. I've promised to find someone's missing phone," said Fiona. "Maybe the following . . ."

She flipped to another page.

"No. The art museum wants me to look at some possible forgeries," she said. "I'm going to have to spend a day or two on research."

She kept flipping.

"Missing cat. Missing backpack. Dog. Cat. Diary. Capybara. Bicycle," Fiona said, combing through her notebook. "How about the end of August?"

"Okay . . . sure," Samantha said, trying not to sound disappointed.

She was a little disappointed, of course. She hoped Fiona might be someone she could eventually share some super secrets with. Maybe Fiona had some secrets of her own.

Fiona looked at the car wash again and then back to Samantha.

"Well . . . bye," she said quickly, "and thanks."

Fiona started up the hill. Samantha watched for a few seconds, and then turned back toward the car wash.

"Wait," Fiona called from behind her.

Samantha turned around again.

"You forgot about the secret door," Fiona said. "The one next to the entrance to the *kogelbaan*. I pointed it out when we first reached the hallway. That's the place I'd look next."

Samantha replayed their adventure in her mind. Fiona was right. It was definitely worth a look, especially now that the whole station smelled like chocolate.

"Thanks," said Samantha. "You really are a master detective."

"I know," said Fiona, and she gave a little nod.

They smiled at each other.

"Good luck with your masterpiece," Fiona added, and began her walk up to Capitol Hill.

Samantha wasn't really sure what Fiona meant, but there wasn't any more time to think about it. Something strange and chocolatey was going on, Nipper was close, and she had to bring him home.

Samantha walked back around to the super-secret entrance, took a deep breath, and tapped the boy in the ball. A blast of warm mist enveloped her, water surged, and she slid under downtown Seattle.

CHAPTER FIFTY-TWO

NICE SNIFF, YOU CAN GET IT

Dennis sniffed.

He smelled the boy!

Sniff, sniff, sniff.

He followed the nice smelly boy.

Up and around and down, down, down the big hill.

He saw an elephant!

No.

It was not a real elephant.

It was a spinning sign.

Sniff, sniff, sniff.

Dennis still smelled the boy.

He smelled something else, too.

Sniff, sniff, sniff!

What's that smell?

Chocolate!

Dennis had smelled it many times.

Dennis had never tasted chocolate.

Good things dropped on the kitchen floor all the time.

Waffles, crackers, granola bars, cereal were delicious.

But when chocolate dropped on the floor, the cone giver always took it away.

The woman who gave him the cone never let him have any chocolate.

Sniff, sniff, sniff!

The boy had chocolate!

The boy always dropped things.

This was his big chance to get chocolate!

Find the boy . . . find the chocolate!
Find the boy . . . find the chocolate!

CHAPTER FIFTY-THREE

TRUTH OR DAREDEVILS

Samantha popped out of the *stroomdroger*.

The smell of chocolate filled the air.

She headed down the hall toward the *kogelbaan*. Before she reached the entrance to the big machine room, she stopped to examine the wall. Two thin lines ran from the floor to the ceiling.

"Secret door," she said.

She pushed slowly, and the rectangular panel creaked open. She leaned in and saw . . . a party?

Streamers dangled from the ceiling of a small chamber. Several dozen balloons drifted by. Men and women in bright blue jumpsuits milled about. Some of them wore red helmets covered in stickers. Others carried red helmets covered in stickers under their arms so they could eat cake.

"Watch out for the CLOUD?" she asked herself quietly.

They didn't seem like much of a danger.

At the far end of the room, beneath a shimmering disco ball, Nipper stood next to a table. Plates of cake cubes, fruit wedges, and marshmallows covered the table. On the other side of him a huge chocolate fountain bubbled. Nipper stabbed at the candy with a wooden skewer and dipped . . . and dipped . . . and dipped.

Samantha walked quickly toward her brother. He didn't notice her at all. His brain had entered the chocolate fountain zone. He dipped a cake cube. He dipped a marshmallow. He skipped the fruit plate. He dipped another cake cube. He stuffed several into his mouth at once.

Someone was standing behind Nipper. The visor screen on the person's helmet was open, and Samantha was pretty sure it was a woman. She wore leather gloves and rubbed them together eagerly as she observed everyone in the room.

Samantha studied the woman's expression. There was something mean about it. Everyone else in the room seemed to be enjoying the party. This woman's eyes darted around, watching everything suspiciously.

Samantha picked up her pace.

Two men in helmets stepped in front of her. Samantha guessed they were men, at least. It was hard to tell with their face masks closed.

"Sorry," one of them said. "The fountain's just for the boy."

"Yeah," said the other one. "We don't get any chocolate fondue. But look what I got for luring the boy into this place."

He held out his hand proudly. On one of his fingers, a ring with a green scorpion blinked. Samantha thought that it looked a lot like the creepy ring that Nipper found in the Temple of Horus when they visited Edfu a while ago. But this one was clearly made of plastic, not emeralds.

Samantha looked past the ring to where Nipper stood by the fountain. He was busy stabbing cake cubes with a stick, dipping them into the fountain, and munching furiously. He wasn't paying any attention to the mean-looking woman behind him. She had moved closer to him, and Samantha could see she held something silver in one hand.

"I don't know why the boss wanted us to bring the boy here," said the first man. "He's super annoying. I think Crash Nitro said something about using him as bait."

The mean woman spotted Samantha . . . and her mouth turned up in an evil grin. She raised her hand

and pointed the shiny metal boomerang at her.

"Watch out, Nipper," Samantha shouted. "We're in danger!"

Nipper looked up.

"What are you talking about, Sam?" he replied. "There's nothing safer than cake."

The woman hurled the boomerang.

Samantha reached for her umbrella.

Swish!

Before she could grab the handle. The silver weapon flashed past her head. Samantha felt a rush of air as it sailed inches from her left ear. She froze.

Zip-zip-zip-zip . . . smack!

The boomerang looped around the room. The woman behind Nipper caught it with one gloved hand.

"You're too late," the woman called to Samantha.

She pointed one edge of the boomerang at Nipper's throat and leered at Samantha.

"Now hand over the umbrella," the woman shouted. "Or I'll send both of you to ride track thirteen . . . forever!"

The edge of the boomerang sparkled in the light of the disco ball over the fountain. Samantha knew from the one she had found earlier that its tip was razor sharp.

Nipper didn't pay any attention to the woman with the boomerang standing behind him. He kept dipping.

CHAPTER FIFTY-FOUR

THE BIG DIPPER

Nipper dipped and dipped.

And dipped.

Chocolate splattered everywhere.

He saw something flash close to his neck.

Whatever.

He had to keep dipping.

He dipped all of the cake cubes.

He skipped the fruit and dipped all of the marshmallows.

He couldn't stop dipping.

A woman stood next to him, shouting.

Sam was there, too.

It didn't matter.

He had to keep dipping.

He reached into the woman's pocket.

He pulled out . . . a piece of candy.

He stabbed it with a stick and dipped it.

Delicious.

He found two more candies in her pocket.

He used his fingers.

Dip.

Dip.

Delicious.

The pocket was empty.

Nipper couldn't stop.

He went back to the fruit plate.

He dipped all the fruit and ate it.

Chocolate drizzled onto his shoes.

He didn't care.

He couldn't stop dipping.

He had to keep dipping.

There wasn't anything left on the table.

What could he dip now?

Nipper reached into a different pocket.

He pulled out something shiny.

Maybe it was a banana.

It didn't matter.

He dipped it, and then he tried to bite it.

Ouch!

He put it back.

Must . . . keep . . . dipping.

Nipper looked for another pocket.

He needed to dip more.

"Hey!" the woman shouted at him.

She grabbed his arm.

"Stop that!" she shouted.

Sam was holding up her red umbrella.

She swung it.

Whack!

Sam knocked something out of the woman's hand.

It clattered to the floor.

Sam was pointing to the door with her umbrella.

"Run, Nipper!" his sister shouted. "Run!"

CHAPTER FIFTY-FIVE

FON-DOOMED

"Run!" Samantha shouted again.

Nipper didn't move. He kept staring at the fountain.

The mean woman grinned at Samantha, then she bent down to retrieve her boomerang.

Samantha lunged at her and grabbed Nipper by the wrist. He was slippery, but she got a good grip.

"Let's go!" she shouted, pulling him away from the table.

But Nipper wouldn't budge. She had pulled him away from crowds and clowns and cascading sewage. She had dragged him through city streets around the world. But fondue-Nipper wasn't movable. It was as if gravity had quintupled beneath him. The berserk power of his chocolate frenzy made him as heavy as an elephant!

The mean woman had stood up. She glared at Samantha with rage.

Samantha took a deep breath. There was only one thing she could do. She held on to Nipper's arm and kicked.

Klang!

Samantha kicked the fountain as hard as she could.

Splat!

It tipped and wobbled for a moment and hit the floor. Chocolate flew everywhere.

It splashed across the table and along the floor. It splattered the mean woman and made her look even more terrifying.

"I said *run!*" Samantha shouted.

"When, Sam?" asked Nipper, looking up from the fountain. "When did you say that?"

Her brother's arm was suddenly flexible again. Normal gravity had returned. The frenzy had lifted. She tugged again, and he budged this time.

"No one's leaving this party!" shouted the mean woman.

"Party?" asked Nipper, looking around. "Who are all these people? What's on the floor everywhere? Is it choco—"

Samantha gripped his arm and ran.

She yanked him away from the wrecked fountain, past several startled partiers, and bolted across the

room. In one hand, she held her umbrella. In the other, she held on tight to her brother's sticky wrist.

"After them!" shrieked the woman.

Samantha heard the sound of sneakers slapping the floor behind her. They were gaining on her. . . .

Samantha glanced back and *Fluh-bomp!* The person behind them slipped on a patch of chocolate and wiped out. She kept running and dragging Nipper. They were almost to the secret door.

"Eee-eee-EEE-NUFF!"

The mean woman let out a tremendous howl. It rose in pitch and filled the room. It was so horrifying that Samantha stopped in her tracks. She couldn't help it.

"Take one more step . . . and you die!" the woman roared again.

Samantha turned around. Her brother did, too.

"Uh-oh," said Nipper. "I just noticed. She has a weapon. It looks sharp."

Samantha looked at the enraged chocolate-splattered woman. Brown covered her clothes and her face. Samantha squinted and took a closer look at the woman's raised hand. Her leather glove was smeared with brown blotches. Chocolate oozed down her arm.

Samantha smiled.

"Keep moving," she told Nipper, and pushed him toward the secret doorway.

"I thought I told you to stop!" the woman yelled.

Samantha looked back at her and waved.

"*Rrrrarrr!*" the woman roared, and hurled the boomerang.

Clunk.

The chocolate-dipped weapon slipped from her gloved hand and fell to the floor.

"I've got them!" shouted a voice.

"I'll get them!" shouted another voice.

Samantha looked left. Two new daredevils in chocolate-splashed jumpsuits lunged at her and Nipper.

She stepped a little to one side.

"Whoa, Nelly!" the men both shouted as they slid past on fondue-slicked sneakers.

Wham!

Samantha watched them skid across the room, slam into the wall, and fall down, unconscious.

"Watch out for the CLOG," said Nipper.

"The CLOG?" Samantha asked.

"Yeah," he replied. "Chocolate-laced, out-cold goofballs."

Samantha smiled at Nipper.

"Good one," she said.

The word *clog* made her think of Uncle Paul and her father. Where did the "Spinner Boys" wind up? And why *did* her uncle basically let her go find Nipper all by herself?

"Come on," she told Nipper. "Let's get out of here."

They stepped over the two men, walked quickly to the secret doorway . . . and stopped.

A tall man in a trench coat blocked the opening.

"*S'il vous plaît*," he said.

With lightning speed, the man pulled out two pairs of metal handcuffs.

Snap! Snap!

He locked one each on Samantha's and Nipper's wrists.

"*Merci*," he said.

Snap-snap!

He locked the other end of each handcuff to his belt and rested a fist on each hip. Samantha and Nipper tugged, but neither could break away. It was even harder than pulling Nipper away from a chocolate fountain.

"You are going . . . no place," he said in a thick French accent.

Samantha tugged again. He was strong. She noticed his silver badge. It was shaped like the Eiffel Tower. The man looked down and saw her staring at it. He smiled.

"Let me make a correction," said the man. "You two international criminals *are* going somewhere. I am taking you back . . . to France!"

CHAPTER FIFTY-SIX

NOT A QUESTION

"Oh, no you don't!" shouted the angry, angry woman. "You can't just storm into *my* headquarters and take away *my* prisoners!"

Samantha saw that she had picked up her boomerang. The woman was now using a clean spot on her jumpsuit sleeve to wipe off the chocolate. Grunting, she crossed the room to Samantha, Nipper, and the tall man.

She pointed a boomerang tip at Samantha and Nipper. She looked Samantha in the eye, glanced at the umbrella, and snickered.

"I'll tell you what, Mr. French Detective," she said. "You can have these two *international criminals*. Just let me keep that girl's umbrella."

Samantha gasped. How did she know?

The man looked at the woman wearing the helmet and then glanced at the umbrella on Samantha's shoulder. He looked at Nipper. He seemed to be thinking it over.

"We have a deal," he said finally, and turned to Samantha. "Hand it over, young American girl."

"Don't worry," the mean woman growled in a fake-friendly voice. "I'll keep your umbrella safe until you come back from France. Any questions?"

"There's something in the hallway," said Samantha.

"That's not a question!" the woman snapped. "Now give me the . . ."

Mechanical noises rumbled through the open doorway. It sounded like someone had turned on a jet engine or a very, very powerful hair dryer.

CHAPTER FIFTY-SEVEN

STROOMDROGER

Maybe he saw a moment for greatness. Maybe he wanted to save his friends. Or maybe it was the smell of melted chocolate that lured Dennis into the *Stroomdroger Voor Kleine Dieren*.

The red beam of the motion sensor swept across his front paws. The buzzer rang twice, and fans roared to life.

Ffff-wup!

The power dryer sucked the pug into its chamber.

Clackity-tak!

Clackity-clackity-tak!

Clackity-clackity-clackity-tak!

Dennis's Blinky Barker light flashed on and off as he barked and tumbled about the glass box, thumping against the sides and clattering.

Clackity-thunk!

His body slid out from the *stroomdroger,* but his cone was too wide to fit through the opening.

"Wruf!" he barked over the sound of high-power blowers.

The mechanical noises started to rise in pitch. They grew louder and louder.

"Wruf!" he barked again.

The air pressure built and built, until . . .

POP!

Rear end first, Dennis shot from the *stroomdroger* like a marshmallow candy from a peanut gun.

CHAPTER FIFTY-EIGHT

FRANCE IN YOUR PLANS

"Dennis!" shouted Samantha and Nipper at the same time.

The pug sailed through the open doorway and slammed into the angry woman, knocking her backward. She hit the floor, and her helmet went flying. Her hair was a wild jungle of bright colors.

"It's the Rainbow Thief!" shouted the detective.

The angry woman with rainbow hair scrambled to her feet and glared at Samantha with fury.

She raised her boomerang above her head.

The French detective pulled the badge from his chest and flung it at the boomerang, knocking it out of the woman's hand.

"Whoa," said Nipper.

Immediately the man unlocked the handcuffs on Samantha and Nipper.

Snap-snap!

He locked both of the woman's hands behind her back.

"I'm in really big trouble, aren't I?" she asked the detective.

"That . . . is a very good question!" he said cheerfully.

"And that's *not* an answer," she muttered.

The man looked at Nipper, who shrank away from him.

"It's okay, young American boy," said the man. "You are free to go."

He looked at Samantha.

"You may go, too," he said. "That woman is an international jewelry thief. I will hand her to the Australian authorities. Then I will return to Paris—as a triumphant crime stopper!"

Samantha wasn't one hundred percent sure what all this was about. But it didn't matter. She had found her brother, and with some help from Dennis, she had saved him. It was time to go home.

She nodded at the tall Frenchman.

"Follow me," she told Nipper. "I bet there's a way out of here without going back through the . . . Dennis!"

By her feet, the hero pug was busy sniffing at a patch of chocolate. He was trying to lick it, but his cone kept his tongue from reaching the floor.

"No, boy," she said, grabbing him by the collar behind the back of his neck and pulling him away from the goo. She picked him up and cradled him. He sniffed at her a few times; then he tried to lick the chocolate-covered rim of his cone. He couldn't reach.

As Samantha watched the pug trying to lick the chocolate, she looked up. All around, the men and women in the jumpsuits stood watching her. Their clothes and faces were splattered with chocolate, but they were all staring right at her. They seemed to be waiting for her to give them directions or something.

She shook her head at them; then she looked at the French detective again. He hummed to himself cheerfully as he went back and forth between adjusting his badge and keeping an eye on his new captured criminal. The song reminded Samantha of music she had heard playing by the entrance to the Eiffel Tower.

Standing beside him, the woman was busy trying to clean smudges of chocolate from her weird rainbow hair. Each time she wiped a lock against her jumpsuit, she just made it worse. Her hair had become a snarl of red, orange, yellow, green, blue, indigo, violet . . . and brown.

"Let's get out of here, Nipper," she said. "This place has chocolate and candy . . . and way too many nuts."

Together, they walked through the secret doorway and started to search for another way out. They'd all had enough *stroomdrogers* for one day.

CHAPTER FIFTY-NINE

HALL'S WELL

Still carrying Dennis, Samantha stood beside her brother and stared at the glass-walled *stroomdroger* chambers.

"I'm not sure how to pass through these in the other direction," she told Nipper.

She scanned the hallway. She wanted to go home. She really hoped Uncle Paul would be there, too. She had added a whole bunch of new notes to her journal today, but she didn't feel any closer to learning *everything*.

"Look, Sam," said Nipper, pointing to one side. "It's another secret door."

Thin lines, barely detectable, formed a rectangle on the wall.

"Nice," said Samantha. "I'm impressed."

"I bet that's another *uitgang*," Nipper told her.

"Now I'm really impressed," said Samantha.

"Well . . . don't get too carried away, Sam," said Nipper. "I have no idea what it means."

She pushed on the wall, and it opened. Beyond, it was so dark, they couldn't see a thing.

Samantha looked down at Dennis. She dropped him on the floor.

"Wruf!" barked the little dog.

Blazing white light shot from his cone, revealing what had been hidden in darkness. Before them was a long narrow hallway that ended in a staircase that led up and out of sight.

"What's that smell?" asked Nipper.

Samantha looked down at Dennis again. Steam rose from the plastic cone. Chocolate simmered from the heat of the intense light.

"Sorry," she said. "Fondue for Fido's forbidden."

"Hold off, Sam," said Nipper. "Save it for when you're back with Uncle Paul."

"Lead on," she said to Dennis, and gestured toward the stairs.

With the super-beacon dog in the lead, they walked down the narrow hall, climbed the steps, and exited to the sidewalk.

Soon, they were heading back up Denny Way.

"Stop!" a voice called from behind them. "Wait for us!"

Samantha turned and saw that the CLOUD had followed them. They were all waving and smiling.

She and Nipper waited for them to catch up.

"Okay," said one of the chocolate-smeared daredevils. "We admit that following Crash—the Rainbow Thief—was a big mistake."

"Yeah," said another. "And that party wasn't fun at all."

"We're going to start over," said a different daredevil.

She held out a fanny pack. She unzipped the top and presented it to Samantha.

"You can have this," she said. "And then you can be our new leader."

Samantha looked at the open pack. Jewelry, gems, and other trinkets sparkled.

"We're going to change our name, too," she added. "We're calling ourselves the Cool League of Daring Skills now."

"The CLODS?" Nipper whispered to Samantha.

Samantha quickly raised her hand and pointed two fingers at her brother. It was the same gesture her mom used to make rodents and lizards stand still. Nipper froze.

Samantha turned back to the group of daredevils. "You don't need a leader," she said, shaking her head. "You have what it takes to do daring skills on your own. And I have to get home . . . and find some answers."

"Yeah," said Nipper. "And you're all out of chocolate anyway."

Samantha handed the fanny pack back to the closest CLOD.

"But it's really important that you return all these stolen things," she told them firmly.

They all nodded eagerly.

"Any questions?" she added.

They all shook their heads at the same time. Samantha could tell that these goofballs really liked following directions. There was a good chance that they were actually going to return the loot.

"Wait," said Nipper.

He reached into the fanny pack and picked out a big blue diamond. It was about the size of a walnut.

"That's mine," he said, holding it up to Samantha. "Remember?"

Samantha nodded. Nipper tucked it into his pocket.

"And I'll take this, too," he said, digging into the fanny pack again.

He pulled out a granola bar.

Dennis started to whimper.

"No, pal," said Nipper. "This is for me, not you."

"Wruf!" barked Dennis.

A bolt of light hit Nipper in the face. He threw up his hands, shielding his eyes, and dropped the granola bar on the ground.

"Wruf!" Dennis barked again, cutting off the super beam.

The pug sprang forward and gobbled the granola.

Samantha watched the CLODS heading back toward the car wash. She felt confident their stolen goods were going to wind up where they belonged. She turned and looked in the direction of Capitol Hill. That was where she and her brother belonged.

"Let's roll," she told him.

"Please, Sam," said Nipper. "I'd like to walk instead."

CHAPTER SIXTY

INVESTIGATIONS, INVITATIONS

When they reached the corner of Thirteenth Avenue and Aloha Street, Samantha saw someone sitting on the fire hydrant. It was Lainey Jain.

"Hi, Sam," Lainey said. "Is that the little brother we were looking for?"

"The one and only," she answered.

They both looked at the chocolate-splattered boy.

"You were right about the whole fondue-fountain-berserk thing," said Samantha.

"Of course," Lainey replied. "I know almost every-thing about little brothers. Some people think I'm just a reciter of useless facts, but little brothers are really interesting. I'm writing a book about all my research and experiences."

Samantha gulped.

"Don't worry," Lainey said. "I'm not going to mention today's adventure. I can tell you want to keep some secrets."

"Secrets?" said Samantha, trying not to seem too concerned. "I don't have super . . . big secrets."

"Maybe," said Lainey. "But it's pretty clear that you and your little brother have been through a lot together."

Lainey studied Nipper for a moment.

"He's probably gotten you into a lot of dangerous situations, too," she observed.

"Well . . . yes," Samantha said carefully.

Lainey sniffed in Nipper's direction.

"Little brothers collect a lot of smells," she said. "They're one of the few things they hardly ever lose."

She sniffed again.

"Cumin . . . and hot pepper," she said. "Maybe spices from an African market?"

Lainey sniffed again.

"Do I smell exhaust from a motorcycle?" she asked.

"I get it," said Samantha, cutting her off.

"Whoops," said Lainey. "I'll try not to mention any of this if you come to my party next week."

Samantha smiled again. She didn't get invited to many parties. She guessed there would probably be a lot of useless facts about little brothers, but also some fun.

"I'll come," said Samantha. "As long as you don't have any chocolate fountains."

Lainey smiled. Then she looked at Nipper, studying his forehead. Samantha guessed she was checking her theory about scars on boys' heads.

"Do you know how you got this scar?" Lainey asked Nipper, pointing to his forehead.

He thought about it, then he shrugged.

"I haven't the foggiest idea," he told her.

"That's just what I thought," said Lainey.

Samantha noticed Lainey had that same wistful expression she'd had earlier.

"You know what I think?" Samantha asked.

"What?" said Lainey.

"I think you really wish that you had a little brother of your own," said Samantha.

Lainey tilted her head. She seemed to ponder this.

"Possibly," said Lainey. "I've never spent a lot of time thinking about it."

Samantha guessed that Lainey had actually spent a lot of time thinking about it. It explained many things.

Lainey stood up off the fire hydrant and smiled.

"Chinchillas are pretty fascinating, too," she said. "See you later."

She turned and left.

"Who was that?" asked Nipper.

"Just a friend," said Samantha. "Sort of."

"I'm really ready to go home, Sam," Nipper said.

"Me too," she replied. "I'm finally going to learn *everything*."

"Sure," said Nipper. "And I might *eat* everything."

The Alhambra

A castle sits high in the mountains of southern Spain.

The Alhambra was first built as a small fortress in 889 and expanded into a royal palace in 1333. The name means "the red fort," in Arabic, because of the rose-colored granite used to construct the original building. Today, the Alhambra is one of Spain's more popular tourist attractions. It is considered a masterpiece of Islamic art and architecture with tiled floors and walls that are marvels of geometry and mathematics.

* * *

Walk to the edge of the main reflecting pool and find the hexagon-shaped tile that is black instead of blue. Press it, and you'll hear a soft scraping sound deep below. It should last for about thirty seconds.

When the sound stops, the *supersonic moonshooter* will be ready to launch you to Norway.

CHAPTER SIXTY-ONE

LATER, CALCULATOR

"If you feel like writing some kind of power-moping gloom journal, there's a pad of paper and a pen in the kitchen," said George Spinner.

"I'm not much of a writer," Paul said.

"Well . . . I was hoping you'd give me a little privacy," said George, picking up his phone. "I've decided to call Suzette. I'm really going to tell her about the dog this time."

"Are you going to mention the boy, too?" asked Paul. "Sooner or later she will notice that you lost both her dog and her—"

Bzzt! Bzzzzzt!

Paul reached under the coffee table and grabbed one of the dog clogs.

Bzzzzt! Bzzt!

Smiling, he held it up so George could see the heel. One word flashed on the readout screen:

_ D _ E _ N _ N _ I _ S _

The front door swung open. Samantha stood there with Nipper beside her. In one hand, she held her umbrella. Tucked under her other arm was Dennis, cone and all.

"Old pal!" exclaimed George.

"Wruf!" barked the pug.

A beam of bright white light blasted Paul, and he fell backward onto the carpet. Samantha dropped the dog and rushed forward to help her uncle.

"I'll take that light source back, thank you," said George.

He reached inside Dennis's cone, unsnapped the cover on the Blinky Barker collar, and removed the high-power lightbulb. The blinding beam stopped.

"Weren't you just about to call Suzette?" said Paul, rubbing his eyes.

Mr. Spinner looked around the room.

"Two kids, one dog," he counted.

He set his phone back on the coffee table.

"She'll be home tomorrow," said George. "She doesn't need any more distractions on her long trip."

Samantha glared at him. She couldn't believe, after all this time, her father had not told her mother that Nipper had gone missing.

"I'm going to put this someplace safe," Samantha said, waving her umbrella at her uncle. "Then it's time to talk about *everything*."

"Yes. This is a perfect time," he replied.

Samantha headed up the stairs.

"Waitaminute," Paul said to George. "An idea just came to me. That girl next door, the one who isn't very nice to Nipper. I think she looks a lot like—"

The doorbell rang.

"Hold that thought," said George, walking across the living room. "I'll get it."

Dennis started growling.

George pulled open the front door.

Two women and two men stood in the doorway, wearing scuffed-up lab coats. All had big bandages on their foreheads.

"Did all of you encounter Horizontally Extending Architectural Dangers?" George asked them.

The four strangers looked at each other and nodded. Then they turned back to George without answering him. One of the women stepped forward. George noticed a formula stitched to the front of her outfit:

$$ax^2 + bx + c = 0$$

"The quadratic equation," George observed.

"Watch out, Dad!" shouted Nipper. "They're the math police!"

"Who?" Paul asked. "What? Are you sure about that?"

The woman reached out and grabbed George by the collar. She held up a shiny metal ruler and pressed it against his throat.

"Mr. Spinner is coming with us," said another one of the strangers.

"Which one?" asked George, being careful not to bump the ruler.

The strangers seemed confused. They exchanged looks with each other. All of the *Mr. Spinners* looked at each other, too.

"Okay, Super Numerical Overachievers," Paul said suddenly.

He stepped forward and took the ruler out of the stranger's hand.

"I'll go with you," he announced.

The four strangers looked at each other. They nodded in unison.

"But wait right here," Paul said quickly. "I have to do something first."

He walked briskly out of the room. George could hear him in the kitchen, opening and closing drawers. A few more seconds passed before Paul reappeared in the living room.

"So long, guys," he said to George and Nipper. "I'll see you in . . . um . . ."

"In 3.14159 weeks," said one of the strangers.

The woman holding the ruler looked at Paul, then back to George.

"Good pi," she said, and closed the door.

George stood beside Nipper in the living room. Neither of them said anything.

The silence was broken by the sound of footsteps as Samantha came down the stairs.

"Did I miss anything?" she asked.

CHAPTER SIXTY-TWO

DON'T BE AWFUL

"I can't believe it," Samantha shouted. "I leave for two minutes and *what* happens? You lose Uncle Paul again!"

She plopped down on the living room sofa. She had learned almost *nothing*.

"Your uncle left with some mathematicians," said her father.

"The math police," said her brother.

"Who?" Samantha asked. "What? Are you sure that's who they were?"

"They had rulers and protractors," said Nipper.

"They wanted a 'Mr. Spinner,'" said her father. "So your uncle volunteered."

"Really?" Samantha asked. "Do you even know

who they were? Do you have any idea where they're taking him?"

"Probably . . . or possibly," said Mr. Spinner. "I think he's going to calculus camp. Maybe."

"But you're not sure?" Samantha asked.

"Well . . . ," said her father. "He agreed to go, and that seemed reasonable. So he made a quick trip to the kitchen. Then he came back here and—"

Samantha held up her hand. Her father stopped talking. She turned to leave.

"Where are you going, Sam?" Nipper asked.

"When things seem awful . . . ," said Samantha.

"Have a waffle," he answered.

"Exactly," she replied, and headed to the kitchen.

She looked at all the shelves and open cabinets, at all the cookbooks stacked around the room in piles.

Samantha half-smiled.

Had her uncle taken them all out so she would notice the school directory? She looked for the little booklet, but it wasn't where she had left it. She spotted it beside the waffle iron. She moved over to it quickly and picked it up.

A mitten lay on the counter underneath the book.

She picked it up and found a note tucked between the thumb and the rest of the mitt:

Watch out for the SNOW!
Uncle Paul

CHAPTER SIXTY-THREE

BRAND-NEW DAY

Samantha slept the whole night without dreaming about ninjas, clowns, daredevils, or missing uncles. She woke up feeling . . . great!

Something smelled delicious. She followed the aroma out of her room, down the stairs, and into the kitchen.

Her father stood over the stove, pouring batter on a round pan.

"Good morning," he said. "Your mother will be here soon, so I thought I'd surprise her with something new."

He flipped a thin, round cake onto a plate.

"Crepes," he said.

Samantha watched her father cook. Her adventures were getting stranger and stranger, but on the bright side, her father was getting better and better at breakfast-making.

"Hi, Sam," said Nipper, walking in through the side door. "I was playing catch with Dennis in the back-yard."

"Let me guess," she said. "You lost the ball."

He smiled weakly.

Samantha sniffed. She smelled something unusual in addition to the crepes—and it wasn't chocolate, dirty socks, glycerol, super-hot cinnamon slush, cumin, hot chili pepper, or sludge from an ancient tomb. Her brother smelled like . . . shampoo!

"You took a bath?" asked Samantha.

She sniffed the air dramatically two more times.

"You really did it," she said. "I can't believe it. That's amazing."

Samantha knew she was laying it on thick, but she wanted to encourage him.

"Yeah, yeah," Nipper replied. "It's part of a whole program. I'm making big new changes in my life."

He pulled up his pant legs to reveal clean socks.

"Great, huh?" he asked.

Samantha smiled. This actually was a great devel-opment. She nodded at him and—

"Wait a minute," she said, looking at his face.

Nipper was chewing with his mouth open.

"What's in your mouth?" she asked.

Nipper opened wide so she could see something colorful on his tongue.

"Oh . . . my . . . gosh!" she gasped. "Are you chewing that *same piece of gum*? You are exceptionally gross!"

"Relax," said Nipper. "That gum's a thousand miles away now. I'm eating marshmallow circus peanuts."

"Really?" said Samantha. "But circus peanuts are the saddest candy of all."

"I listened to you, Sam," he said cheerfully. "You were right. I've been too much of a picky eater. Picky eater, picky eater."

"Picky eater?" she asked. "I didn't say anything about that. Who said you were a picky eater?"

"From here on in, I'm making big changes in my life," Nipper continued. "I'm learning to love *all* kinds of snacks."

Samantha shook her head. Her brother was a goofball. She had just saved a goofball from being captured by a bunch of goofballs.

"Loving all kinds of snacks doesn't seem like a big change to me," she told him.

"And now . . . ," he said dramatically, "I'm going next door. I have a plan!"

"Again?" said Samantha. "That's not a big new change, either. You do this almost every . . ."

But her brother had already left the kitchen through the side door.

CHAPTER SIXTY-FOUR

BRONX BUMMERS

Nipper skipped cheerfully, enjoying the beautiful morning. The sky was clear, and the sun was shining. It felt good to be outside. He took in a deep breath of fresh air as he hopped over the hedge. What a great day.

As he headed up the drive to the Snoddgrass side porch, he noticed two adults looking out a window on the second floor. They smiled and waved at him. It was weird, but he didn't care. Today was a great day. Today he was going to get his Yankees back.

Nipper reached out to knock on the screen door. Before he could, the inside door swung open and Missy Snoddgrass pushed the screen door out, forcing Nipper to jump back.

"Hello, Jeremy Bernard Spinner," she said quickly. "Did you get a haircut recently?"

Nipper felt the patch where the math police's flying blade had sliced his hair. Missy sure paid attention to details—especially when they were details about him getting attacked! He decided to ignore the question, and kept smiling.

"Okay, Missy," he said cheerfully. "Let's just pretend none of that yarn stuff happened. I'm here to make a deal with you."

Missy folded her arms and stared at him.

Nipper reached into his pocket.

"This time, I know I've got something you'll want," he continued. "If you give me my Yankees back, you can keep this, and we can just . . . we can just . . ."

He fumbled in his pocket for a few seconds. Empty. He checked his other pocket. The big blue diamond was gone!

"Are you looking for something?" she asked, waving a walnut-sized gem.

"Hey! That's mine!" Nipper cried.

"Not anymore," said Missy, dropping the gem into the front pocket of her yellow-polka-dot blouse. "Besides, I'm not sure that embarrassing excuse for a baseball team is worth so much of your time and energy. They only have a few games to go until it all comes to an end—for good."

"For good?" asked Nipper. "What does that mean— *for good*?"

Missy took a page from her pocket, unfolded it, and read.

" 'Major League Baseball, Rule number 1313, Section 13. *Team liquidation,*' " she read. " 'In the event that any team loses 150 games in a row, the club shall be canceled permanently. All of their bats shall be chopped up for firewood, and uniforms shall be donated to regional theaters for baseball-related musical productions.' "

"Liquidation? Firewood? Theater?" Nipper exclaimed. "Let me see those rules."

He reached out to grab the page from her.

Missy pulled it back quickly and used her free hand to grab three of Nipper's fingers. She twisted them, and a jolt of pain shot through his wrist.

"Ouch!" Nipper wailed.

Missy let go of his fingers and shoved him off the porch.

"If you get close to me again, Jeremy Bernard Spinner, more than a few rules are going to get broken," she growled.

She paused and did a quick calculation in her head.

"Two hundred and six of them," she snapped.

Missy pointed at the driveway.

"Now, get out of here!" she ordered.

00000000010000020020010000081001000006010051010020
00000000000000030030060?000000000

Nipper looked up at the second floor of Missy's house. The grown-ups in the window were smiling. The man was using his tie to wave at him. The woman held up a plate of cookies and nodded. This was strange and creepy . . . and there were cookies. But Nipper wasn't interested right now. His Yankees were still gone.

He let out a long heavy sigh and lowered his head.

Nipper didn't feel like hopping over the bushes. He trudged down the Snoddgrass driveway, turned right at the sidewalk, and slunk home.

When he got to the front door, he stopped and looked down. A large envelope lay on the doormat.

He picked it up and went inside.

CHAPTER SIXTY-FIVE

LIGHTS OUT

"Sam!" Nipper shouted as he slammed the door behind him. "I still lost my— Oh, never mind."

Samantha looked up from the couch. She saw the front door opening again behind Nipper.

"Mission accomplished," said Dr. Spinner, walking through the door and putting down her suitcase.

Both kids rushed to give their mother a big hug.

"Hello, Suzette," Samantha's father called as he entered from the kitchen. "I've been working on something while you've been gone."

"Just a minute, George," said Dr. Spinner.

She handed something shiny to Samantha. It was a sparkling pink envelope with handwritten letters in gold ink.

"Buffy gave this to me when I left her at the airport," said Dr. Spinner. "It's for you. She made me promise not to open it before I got home."

Samantha opened the envelope. Glitter spilled out onto the carpet. She unfolded a single sparkling page and read it out loud.

"'Dearest Mother, Father, Sammy, and little baby Nipper. I have wonderful news.'"

"I'm not a baby," said Nipper.

"'It looked like I was going to have to abandon my dreams and go back to being a dreary high school student in California,'" Samantha continued. "'Thank goodness I listened to my amazing mother's advice . . . forget school, make a movie.'"

Samantha glanced at her mother, who looked alarmed.

"'And then I remembered,'" Samantha kept reading. "'Sometimes people make movies in California!'"

"Isn't that why she went there in the first place?" asked Mr. Spinner.

"'*Scarlett Hydrangea's Wild, Wild Secret of the Nile*,'" Samantha read. "'I'm going to turn my show into a fabulous musical nature documentary!'"

"A musical nature documentary?" Samantha repeated.

Bzzt! Zzzzzzzzzzzt!
Bzzt! Zzzzzzzzzzzt!

On the floor by the sofa, both dog clogs shook.

"Whoops," said Mr. Spinner. "I forgot to deactivate my clogs."

Dr. Spinner picked up one of the shoes.

"Look," she said, holding it so everyone could see the heel.

The display screen lit up with one word:

_ B _ U _ T _ T _ O _ N _

"How is this even possible?" said Mr. Spinner. "The oldest dog ever lived to be only twenty-nine years and five—"

"That's a cool shoe, Dad," Nipper interrupted. "Did you use it to try to find me?"

"Wait," her mother snapped. "Find you?"

"Yeah," said Nipper. "I was lost all over the place."

Samantha watched her mother's face turn bubble-gum pink.

"Did you know there's an elephant building in Margate City?" Nipper continued. "There's a big coffee pot there, too. Or maybe that was in Bedford."

"New Jersey, George?" asked Dr. Spinner. "Pennsylvania, George?"

"I can explain," said her father.

"Nobody can explain Pennsylvania!" her mother shouted.

Samantha knew that if her mother was saying ridiculous things like that, she must be *really, really mad* at her dad! She waved to Nipper to give their parents some time by themselves. She waved for Dennis to follow, and they retreated to the kitchen.

"Hey, Sam," said Nipper. "I meant to thank you for finding me and rescuing me."

Samantha smiled.

"Even though the CLOUD mostly just wanted to give me candy and get me to do dumb things," he added.

Samantha still smiled, but not quite as much. She noticed her brother was holding a manila envelope.

"What's that you're holding?" she asked him.

"What? Oh . . . that. I almost forgot," he answered. "This was outside the front door. I found it when I came home from not getting my Yankees back again."

Nipper raised the envelope and read the address on the front.

"It's addressed to Camp Pythagoras," he said.

He looked at the letter again.

"It was sent by the Parents of Nipper Spinner," he said.

He looked at the letter once more. There were no stamps!

"There aren't any stamps on it," he said, realizing what that meant. "This letter was returned. It wasn't delivered."

His eyes grew wide.

"Sam! My application never made it to Camp Pythagoras!" he shouted.

"What?" asked Samantha.

"I was never signed up for calculus camp!" he said, so gleefully that it sounded like he was singing. "I'm free, I'm free!"

Nipper threw the letter on the ground and started dancing, swinging his arms and legs back and forth, waggling his fingers and tapping his toes.

Samantha couldn't decide if her brother was doing a weird version of the hokey-pokey or an imitation of a chicken.

"Waitaminute, waitaminute!" she shouted.

Nipper stopped dancing.

"If you weren't signed up for math camp, then *who* took Uncle Paul?" she asked.

Nipper shrugged.

"I don't know," he said. "They had numbers, so I thought they were from math camp."

"You lost Uncle Paul!" Samantha blurted.

She put her head in her hands and looked down and spotted the annoying, sparkly invitation from Buffy on the counter.

Samantha picked it up and turned it over. There was writing on the back of the invitation, too:

P.S.: I met a cute boy at the airport. He's going to meet me in California and help me make my movie! I'm in love!

Buffy had taped a shiny two-by-two print from a photo booth to the back of the invitation. In each of the four pictures, Buffy sat next to a boy, grinning and waving. He wore a big smile and a yellow cap with the words *Pacific Pandemonium* on the front.

Seydou!

She froze.

She tried to say something, but no air came out.

Samantha stared at the photo of her sister next to Seydou in a photo booth. Her vision became blurry. The room started to spin.

"Wruf!" she heard Dennis bark.

The floor zoomed up and hit Samantha . . . or maybe it was the other way around.

Everything went black.

ALAS, NIPPER DIDN'T KNOW THESE

AMAZING FACTS!

- In the 1800s, mustache spoons were popular with gentlemen sporting fancy mustaches. An extra curved part on the spoon kept soup and other food from sticking to facial hair. Today, an antique silver mustache spoon can sell for as much as $5,000.

- Wacky Packages, or "Wacky Packs," are stickers that make fun of household products. First-edition stickers, such as "Crust Toothpaste" or "Quacker Oats," are prized by collectors. A complete original set from 1967 sold for more than $11,400.

- Very few silver dollars from 1895 can be found these days. If you own one in good condition, it could be worth $30,000 or more. (A child's bus fare from Collinsville to St. Louis costs one dollar.)

- The silver 1973 Mercedes 350SL and the white 1970 Porsche 910 are toy Matchbox cars that can cost as much as real cars! If you find one of these in mint condition—without any paint flaked off—it might be worth more than $50,000.

- Baseballs autographed by the great New York Yankee Babe Ruth are rare and very valuable. One of them sold for more than $250,000.

- The Breguet Number 160 Grand Complication pocket watch is more commonly known as the "Marie Antoinette." It took Swiss watch makers forty-five years to complete, and it is the most expensive watch ever built. The value is estimated at $30,000,000.

WHOA, NELLY! THIS BOOK IS FULL OF

SUPER-SECRET SECRETS

You've probably guessed that this book is full of super secrets. So take a closer look at things and find these hidden puzzles and codes:

An Important Message: Do you remember the secret word searches in *Samantha Spinner and the Super-Secret Plans* and *Samantha Spinner and the Spectacular Specs*? Try the same trick here! Copy all the ID letters that appear at the start of Samantha's journal entries. Put them in order, and they will spell out something you should know.

The Snoddgrass Code: Once again, there is a secret message hidden in everything Missy says. Follow the numbers at the bottom of every page where she speaks. There's one digit for each of her words. The number tells you which letter to look at in the word. For example, the number 3 and the word *the* means the letter *E*. If the number is 0, there's no letter for that word.

The Umbrella/Hand Lens Enigma Continues: Each chapter has umbrellas and/or hand lenses at the beginning. It turns out there's a point to them. A *point*. Get it?

Use these super-secret decoders to discover the message.

This is R, for example. (The handle is pointing to the right and the tip is pointing to R.)

This is K. (The handle is pointing to the left and the tip is pointing to K.)

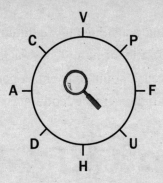

And this is *U*. (The handle is pointing to *U*.)

To learn more about all these puzzles, and a whole lot more secrets, go to samanthaspinner.com.

And if you can't get to a computer, or just want some help, keep reading!

SUPER-SECRET ANSWERS

Everyone needs a little help sometimes!

Here are the answers to the puzzles

hidden in this book.

AN IMPORTANT MESSAGE

The Puzzle:

If you put all the journal entry IDs together in order, they will spell:

DONT W4ST3 YOUR T1M3 LOOK1NG FOR S3CR3T CLU3S
H3R3

TH3R3 H4SNT B33N 4 M3SS4G3 H1DD3N TH1S W4Y

S1NC3 TH3 F1RST BOOK 1N TH3 S3R13S

Now replace all the numbers with letters:

Change every 4 to an A.
Change every 3 to an E.
Change every 1 to an I.
Change every 0 to an O.

The Answer:

The complete message is:

DONT WASTE YOUR TIME LOOKING FOR SECRET
CLUES HERE
THERE HASN'T BEEN A MESSAGE HIDDEN THIS
WAY SINCE THE FIRST BOOK IN THE SERIES

LE MAP

The Puzzle:

Look at Détective Goulot's map. It shows all the cities
he visited looking for Samantha and Nipper. Draw lines
from city to city, following the route he describes in
the text. The lines you draw will cross out most of the
words to reveal a message.

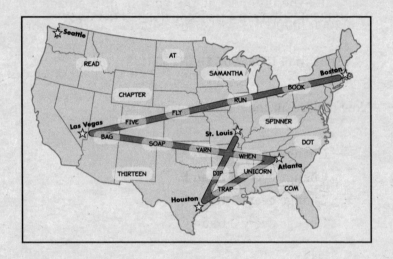

The Answer:

The complete message is:

CHAPTER THIRTEEN AT
SAMANTHA SPINNER DOT COM

THE SNODDGRASS CODE

The Puzzle:

At the bottom of any page where Missy speaks, you will find a row of numbers. Each number signifies which letter in each of Missy's words to keep. For example, when Missy says: "Jeremy Bernard Spinnner," called a voice. "Stop bothering my bird. You're going to wear her out." the numbers at the bottom of the page are 6003000300000. Each digit coincides with a word Missy says. The number refers to the position of the letter in that word to use to solve the puzzle. For example, 6 means the sixth letter of the word, and 0 means no letter. Thus, the hidden word in this example is Y-O-U.

The Answer:

The complete message is:

YOU ARE SO PATIENT SO HERE IS A BIG HINT
GO TO MY WEBSITE AND FIND THE OCTOPUS
WHEN YOU SEE A MAN NAMED CRAIG
REMEMBER HIS LAST NAME
THAT IS A CLUE TO LEARN ABOUT THE WIND

THE UMBRELLA/HAND LENS ENIGMA CONTINUES

The Puzzle:
Just like in books one and two, every chapter in this book has illustrations of umbrellas and/or hand lenses. If you can decode them, you'll find that they continue the secret message that started in the first book.

Depending on which way each one is oriented and which way the umbrella handles are pointed, each drawing secretly represents a letter. (To decode them, use the wheels on pages 310 and 311.)

When you're finished, add this message to the one you found in the last book. A double-triple super-secret development in the Spinner saga will be revealed!

The Answer:
NELLY MCPEPPER AND HER TEAM HAVE TRAVELLED TO SOUTH AFRICA. THEY ARE BUILDING A SPECIAL SUBMARINE AND PRACTICING THEIR SCUBA DIVING SKILLS

ACKNOWLEDGMENTS

Once again, I want to *acknowledge* Team Spinner: **Krista Marino, Kevin O'Connor,** and **Kelly Schrum.** These stories are the result of a four-person creative collaboration. Sam and Nipper wouldn't exist without you. I'm also grateful for an umbrella lining's worth of ideas and advice from my mother, **Carole Karp.**

And . . . oh! What a mistake it would be if I didn't *acknowledge* some people who have been really encouraging and have helped me to get Samantha out into the world. Thanks for singing the theme song just right, **Marianna Previti.** Thanks for making a robotic fish that plays the theme song, **Paul Labys.** Thanks, **Bob Hirshon** and **Laura Nelson,** for helping me drag the Spinner spinner wheel around town.

Special thanks to **Tony Vecchione,** for getting me to write the line "In her heart, Samantha knew that if there was a book written about her, the next chapter would be called It Wasn't Fair." Many kids have told me that it's their favorite line of all. It lets them know that they are in on the joke, and it helps show how it's fun to be smart.

PICTURE CREDITS

Cindy. "An Italian invention called a Motorouta." July 20, 1927. *Motorcycling Magazine*. Web. October 14, 2019.

Denyer, Tristan. "Collinsville water tower." September 23, 2007. Wikimedia Commons. Web. October 14, 2019.

Dethistoricaler. "Uniroyal Giant Tire2015." August 2015. Wikimedia Commons. Web. October 14, 2019. commons.wikimedia.org/wiki/File:UniroyalGiant Tire2015.jpg.

Filitz, Sonja. "Adult hand purposefully holds a ball over a marble run, toy." Digital image. Shutterstock. Web. October 14, 2019.

Goddard, J. T. *The Velocipede: Its History, Varieties, and Practice*. New York: Hurd and Houghton, 1869.

Hamby, Chris. "Hess triangle." December 21, 2012. Flickr. Web. October 14, 2019.

Jebulon. Dawn "Charles V Palace Alhambra Granada Andalusia Spain." August 6, 2014. Wikimedia Commons. Web. October 14, 2019.

Kubina, Jeff. "The Coffee Pot." September 20, 2008. Wikimedia Commons. Web. October 14, 2019.

Mabel, Joe. "Seattle—Elephant Car Wash 02." September 14, 2007. Wikimedia Commons. Web. October 14, 2019.

Nationaal Archief. "One-wheel motorcycle Goventosa." Beeldbank. December 18, 2009. Web. October 14, 2019.

[Photograph of Davide Cislaghi in Milan, Italy, 1924 with an early version]. Digital image. Imgur. Web. October 14, 2019.

Porges, Larry. "Cawker City, KS/USA—September 28, 2015: The world's largest ball of sisal twine sits proudly under a protective canopy in Cawker City, KS." Digital image. Shutterstock. Web. October 14, 2019.

Rattlhed. "Space Needle 002." September 26, 2006. Wikimedia Commons. Web. October 14, 2019.

Sohm, Joseph. "February 2005—Exterior of Corn Palace, roadside attraction in West Mitchell, SD." Digital image. Shutterstock. Web. October 14, 2019.

Sykes, Bev. "St. Louis Gateway Arch." April 14, 2005. Flickr. Web. October 14, 2019.

TigerPaw2154. "TwineBallCawkerKs." July 9, 2013. Wikimedia. Web. October 14, 2019.

wk1003mike. "Toy for kids—Marble ball race game isolated on white background." Digital image. Shutterstock. Web. October 14, 2019.

wk1003mike. "Toy for kids—Marble ball race game isolated on white background." Digital image. Shutterstock. Web. October 14, 2019.

READY FOR INTERNATIONAL INTRIGUE, MANIAC MONKEYS, AND PUZZLING PAJAMAS?

Turn the page for a sneak peek at Samantha's next adventure.

RUSSELL GINNS

SAMANTHA SPINNER

AND THE

PERPLEXING PANTS

MORNING, WARMING . . . WARNING!

Samantha's eyes snapped open.

"Where's Uncle Paul?" she shouted.

She looked around. She was in her room, alone.

She sniffed.

The scent of fresh-baked waffles filled the air.

Had Uncle Paul made breakfast?

No. It was her father downstairs in the kitchen. Of course it wasn't her uncle.

Uncle Paul was missing . . . again.

A little over a week ago, Samantha had found her uncle. She'd had to defeat ninjas, clowns, and daredevils to do it. Then, when she hadn't been around—the moment she'd turned her back—Uncle Paul had gotten taken . . . again!

It was Nipper's fault, and her father's fault, too.

She'd literally just gone upstairs, and a bunch of men and women in white coats and bright white sneakers had showed up at the house . . . and Nipper and her father had let them take her uncle away.

Again!

Nipper had said they were the "math police." But Uncle Paul had left behind an old, worn mitten and a note that said *Watch out for the SNOW!*

Samantha didn't know much more than that. The only thing she had learned from what had happened was that her brother and her father weren't much help at all, especially when it came to not losing Uncle Paul.

She sat up in bed and wiped sweat from her forehead.

Why was it so hot in the house?

She took in her surroundings. Her red umbrella rested against the side of her desk. She hadn't touched it for a week, not since her embarrassing fainting spell.

Samantha had blacked out right after Uncle Paul had been taken away. The doctor said it was due to travel stress, plus a severe attack of *coulrophobia,* a fear of clowns.

Samantha thought *that* was a bunch of hooey. She loved to travel. She had also defeated a band of awful clowns known as the Society of Universal Nonsense. That proved beyond the shadow of a doubt that she wasn't afraid of clowns.

Samantha's mother said her blackout could also have been caused by the shock of seeing Buffy in a photo with a cute new boyfriend. And it was true that Samantha had been shocked. Her sister was completely awful. It didn't make sense that the boy who had saved Samantha and Nipper in Africa had suddenly shown up in California. And it made even less sense that he was there with Buffy.

But what did her mother know about those things, anyway? Dr. Spinner *was* a doctor, but all her patients were rodents and lizards.

It didn't matter. Samantha had slept, rested, and thought about missing uncles, annoying brothers, unhelpful fathers, and ridiculous selfish older sisters for a solid week. It was time to make new plans. And time to find Uncle Paul once and for all.

But that was hard to do when it was so *hot* in the house.

She got up and went to the window. She pulled it open, and a cool, fresh, Seattle summertime breeze wafted into her room.

Much better.

Samantha saw her brother in the backyard, making his way to the house. They hadn't spoken much to each other in the past seven days. At first it was because Samantha had fainted and stayed in bed for a day and a half. Then it was because he wouldn't apologize for letting the people in white coats take Uncle Paul away.

"Watch out for the SNOW," she repeated now.

Was the SNOW the people who had taken her uncle away? Who could they be, and why had they done it?

She had spent enough time resting, and moping. It was time to figure things out. She got dressed and opened her bedroom door. A gust of warm air rolled in from the rest of the house.

Breakfast smelled delicious. And she was ready to talk to Nipper again, even without his apology. She would let him rattle on about his baseball team, and then they could start making plans to save their uncle from the SNOW.

WEATHER OR NOT

"Dad," Samantha called as she walked into the kitchen. "Why is it so hot in here?"

Her father stood at the counter, adjusting the controls of the waffle iron. He wore the yellow mitten from Uncle Paul on his right hand, and he held a pair of waffle tongs in his left. A six-high stack of waffles rested on a plate nearby.

"And why aren't you using an oven mitt?" she added.

"All the oven mitts are missing," he answered. "It's a good thing Paul left us this mitten."

Dennis sat on the floor, close to the kitchen table. He looked wilted. His head drooped inside his plastic cone. The temperature was too much for the little pug.

"Why is it so hot in here?" she asked again.

"Your mother and I decided to turn up the heat," her father said as he poured batter onto the waffle iron. "The radio warned about a cold snap this afternoon."

"Cold snap?" asked Samantha. "Have you looked outside? It's warm and sunny."

"We also got a text alert about a blizzard coming," said Mr. Spinner.

"A text alert?" asked Samantha. "Who sent that?"

"It came from the Storm Notifications of Oregon and Washington," he answered.

"Storm Notification of . . . I've never heard of . . . ," said Samantha. "Wait! Did they call themselves the SNOW?"

"Possibly," said Mr. Spinner. "The alert sounded very serious."

He closed the waffle iron and stepped back from the counter. Then he took a handkerchief from his pocket and mopped his brow.

"But you're right," he said. "It's quite hot in here."

"Where's Mom?" asked Samantha.

"Your mother went to the store to pick up an ice scraper. Just in case," said Mr. Spinner. "She's stopping at her clinic on the way home. Half her patients are cold-blooded, you know."

"I know," said Samantha.

Nipper entered through the back door and stopped in his tracks.

"Whoa!" he said. "Why is it so incredibly hot in here?"

"Okay, you've convinced me," said Mr. Spinner, pulling off the mitten and handing it to Samantha. "Take over while I go turn off the heat."

Before she put it on, Samantha noticed that something was trickling out of the mitten. She let a little bit collect in her open palm. It looked and felt like sand, but it was white.

"Salt?" she asked.

"I prefer my waffles unsalted, thank you very much," Nipper said, sitting down at the table.

Samantha tossed the mitten onto the counter. Then she carried the plate full of fresh waffles to the table. Nipper watched eagerly, but she didn't set it down.

"I need your help finding Uncle Paul," she told him. "So I have a deal for you."

She waved the plate of waffles in front of his face.

"I'll give you all these waffles. Unsalted. Then we start making a plan to find Uncle Paul. Along the way, you can complain about the Yankees losing . . . for a whole five minutes."

Nipper bit his lip. He seemed to be considering it.

"Fifteen minutes?" he asked.

"Okay. Fifteen. That's the maximum time limit, though," said Samantha.

Nipper sniffed the air.

"Can I complain a bit about the waffle that's starting to burn over there, too?" he asked.

Samantha turned to see smoke billowing from the waffle iron on the counter. She dropped the plate in front of her brother and dashed to the counter. She picked up the mitten, put it on, and lifted the lid to the waffle iron. With her other hand, she used the tongs to save the waffle. It was still mostly golden brown.

"Yes, Nipper," she said. "It includes this— Ouch!"

The hot lid touched her hand through a hole in the faded yellow mitten. She loosened her grip on the tongs, and the waffle fell to the floor.

"Wruf!" barked Dennis, suddenly alert.

The Spinners' pug darted across the floor, grabbed the waffle, and disappeared through the doorway. Samantha heard his plastic cone rattling down the hall.

She set down the tongs, removed the mitten, and examined her hand.

The waffle iron lid wasn't hot enough to have burned her badly, but it had left a little red mark on the edge of her right palm, just below her thumb.

She carried the mitten over to Nipper and sat down next to him.

"See this hole?" she asked, pointing to a tiny circle below the thumb. "I think Uncle Paul made this on purpose."

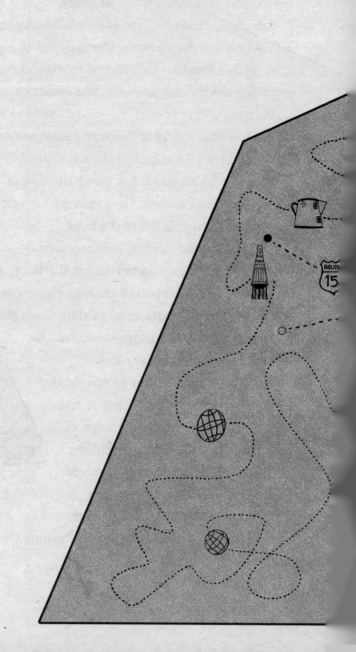

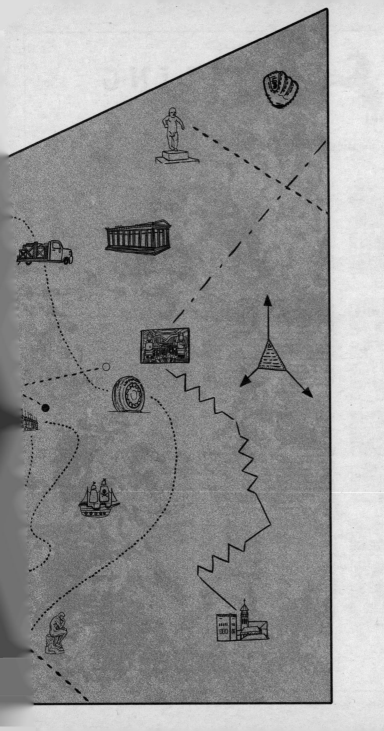

1291